REMEMBERING TO SAY 'MOUTH' OR 'FACE'

Stories by
Omar S. Castañeda

FICTION
COLLECTIVE
T W O

BOULDER • NORMAL

REMEMBERING TO SAY 'MOUTH' OR 'FACE'

This book is the winner of the 1993 Charles H. and N. Mildred Nilon Excellence in
Minority Fiction Award, sponsored by the University of Colorado and Fiction
Collective Two

Published jointly by the University of Colorado and Fiction Collective Two with
assistance from the National Endowment for the Arts and the Illinois Arts Council
and the support of the Publications Center of the University of Colorado at Boulder
and the English Department Publications Unit at Illinois State University

Address all inquiries to: Fiction Collective Two, Publications Center, Campus Box
494, University of Colorado, Boulder, CO 80309-0494

Remembering to Say 'Mouth' or 'Face'
Omar S. Castañeda

PS
3553
A8133
A6
1993

ISBN: Cloth, 0-932511-80-5, $18.95
ISBN: Paper, 0-932511-81-3, $8.95

Manufactured in the United States of America
Distributed by The Talman Company

CONTENTS

ON THE WAY OUT

CROSSING THE BORDER

REMEMBERING

For my mother and father,
Miriam Méndez Castañeda and Hector Neri Castañeda

ACKNOWLEDGMENTS

The following stories first appeared in:
"On the Way" in *The Kenyon Review*; "I Tell You This" in *Five Fingers Review*; "Woman of the Bus" in *Left Bank*; "Shell and Bone" in *New Visions: Fiction by Florida Writers*; "Under and Ice Moon" in *G.W. Review*; "Crossing the Border" in *Blue Light/Red Light*; "Vanguard of Wood" in *Five Fingers Review*; "Along a Black Road West" in *Caliban*; "A Matter of Twins" in *The Kenyon Review*; "The Sad History of the False Sun and Moon" in *Mid-American Review*; and "The North Is White" in *Imagine*.

This work owes much to the English translations of the *Popol Vuh* by Munro S. Edmonson and Dennis Tedlock. Interested readers should consult both works as well as the Spanish translation by Adrián I. Chávez, *Pop Wuj*.

At Dusty Court, the twins discovered the faces of their fathers. High above them like moribund fruit, 1 Blowgunner's head swayed, his mind somewhere already disassembling and losing information on its way toward that entropic sea. 7 Blowgunner spread away along the ground like a mist leaking across, drifting off from undulating reeds.

"Name yourselves," the sons said. "Fathers, quickly!"

Lazily the wind swirled; the head tried to recall the manner of its life. "7 Blowgunner," it said, but it wasn't really speaking. There was a mumbling, an incomprehension, an apish chatter, not true language.

1 Blowgunner was asked the name of everything: his nose, the socket of his eye. "Eye, my sons." But he could not name the lips of his mouth, nor the tongue inside his head.

The twins wept for their fathers in the tree and on the ground at Dusty Court.

"Your forms will be left here," they said. "You will be called for in the future. The light born, the light engendered, will call out your names."

—Popol Vuh

ON THE WAY OUT

ON THE WAY OUT

Long before I am supposed to die, I learn all there is to learn about swearing from my mother. She slams a door against her side as she struggles in with groceries and it's *"Hijo de la gran perica."* In Spanish it is deliberately goofy: "Son of the great/grand parrot." In English it is preposterous; it has no hint of several puns. In English my mother sounds like something gone awry.

"Gahd-dahm eat," she says when she remembers that she is in the Ju-knighted Estates.

We know all about when she first came to the Ju-knighted Estates and she had to go and buy bedsheets in a Midwestern Sears. The boy said "What?" fifteen times. "De sheet depar-ment," my mother says she said. He directed her down the hall, right, left at the fountain, then straight ahead, where she walked up to the bathroom displays. My mother's face gets red as a hot-house tomato when she tells this, she laughs so hard. She says, "I'll going to *orinar* in my undergwear," and laughs harder, hands clasping her abdomen.

She has been in this country for twenty-two years when I am supposed to die.

"Hey, Pancho," she says to us, her children. This is better than when she wants to call one of us by his proper name because we have to wait until she names every other name before finally saying, "Ju, Gahd-dahm eat, whoteber jour name ease—Pancho! Where are ju going?"

"Out, Mother." Always out. Away. A friend's. The store. Out: Out, spot, out!

Always out. There are eight of us.

Then I'm gone for years in the service because I get this lady pregnant and I want to do the right thing. "Fack," my mother says. "Fack, fack!" But I go. I get out of high school. I get married. I join the Air Force. I want my life to sound like English. American English.

And in two years my wife sleeps with every serviceman in Okinawa. I want to keep this thing going because America has nuclear families and we have one child and two swimming upstream in tandem. I, of course, don't know this until later, when her belly has some kind of calabash inside that the doctor identifies. She has long ago stopped coming home so I ask, "Are they mine?"

"How can you ask such a thing? How can you think that I would sleep with another man?"

I hold a piece of the beige curtain as I look out. There is a line of men winding away into the starlit night. One of the men is holding photographic equipment: the old kind, with hood and clumsy tripod. There is Columbian music coming from somewhere.

"I just want to know."

"God! You're so jealous! You're always thinking I'm cheating on you. I may as well cheat on you, if you think that!"

"I'll still love the twins."

She is smoking so much that I can barely see her head. There is a cigarette in each ear and one in each nostril. Her mouth is pulling on another.

"What do you want to do?"

She stabs out the cigarette from her mouth on the kitchen cutting board. "I want to be trusted." She throws up her hands and sighs. "I just want to have a normal life."

I think that that's what I want. That I grew up getting the shit beat out of me because I was a wet-back spick. I had boys tie me up in trees and spit in my face because I spoke Spanish. I wanted to go to school and not have the entire class laugh and throw things because of the teacher's inability to pronounce my name. I wanted people to say Hernández: Err-NAN-dez with a straight face. I wanted to have an end to names like Hernia, Her-nuts, Hernia-daze, Wet-back, Speak Spickish.

"I want what you want," I say.

"Let me in peace, then." And she kisses our sleeping daughter on the forehead and gets ready for her church meeting.

I watch her shave her pussy with one leg propped up on the toilet.

"When will the meeting end?"

"How do I know?" she says. She is sighing again.

"Should I wait up for you?"

"Do what you like." She washes the shaving cream off in the sink and powders herself with Johnson's Baby Powder. "I'll try and make it home before Ann gets up."

I insist on the name Ann. My wife wants to name her Apricot or Zarzuela. I say, "Holy cow! I suffered through Hermanegildo and my kid is not suffering like I did." But I don't say it there and then as I watch her smooth black stockings up to the violet garter snaps. That's just one of those goofy things with present tense. Instead, I say, "It would be nice for all of us to have breakfast together."

Violet smiles largely. She wiggles into a taffeta dress, and twirls so that the hem swirls up to where panties would be revealed had she worn any. "Yeah," she says.

I'm not sure what she is referring to. "Yeah, what?"

"Yeah," she says. She shoos me out the bedroom door so she can make a call while she puts on makeup.

I don't know why, but during these years of marital trouble, I begin to shoot a little heroin. I punch the needle through my skin and fire the scag. When I'm off, my laughter feels like it is a tree blossoming out from my mouth, the branches full of birds and chattering squirrels. The bole is smooth like a birch or, better, like an aspen. But what I enjoy most is that the laughter has roots that entwine their dendritic ends into every vein and capillary of my body.

It isn't long before I discover that I can dance a kind of tango with my blood. I cut away the top of the disposable syringe and use a rubber band to secure a plastic cherry on the end.

How to tango, you ask? Easy:

1) Heat the scag in a spoon with 1-100 cc of water, depending on how much you're hitting and how much you like to boot;

2) As you look at the serene pond in the spoon, tie yourself off with a rubber hose, scarf, thin belt, twine, someone else's hand, electric cord, or, if you're hitting somewhere other than your arm, use your own hand;

3) Roll a tiny wad of cotton onto the tip of the needle, making sure to cover the hole (this is for filtering, which shouldn't be necessary if the stuff's good and the water's clean—it's just habit);

4) Depress cherry and hold;

5) Insert point into liquid;

6) Slowly allow cherry to inflate and suck up ALL!—every last microscopic drop!—liquid;

7) Remove cotton ball and eat;

8) Lick spoon;

9) Being careful not to allow liquid to flow back up into the cherry, and making sure vein is bulging, slowly allow the sharp point to pierce the tissue and rip its way to the engorged vein, softly throbbing;

10) You'll know it, you'll know, when it penetrates the thin casing of the vein—a minuscule storm of blood will roil up into the syringe, blossoming and billowing like a wondrous spring storm that turns everything crystalline in its wake, clean, vibrant and bright with sun;

11) I prefer to untie at this point—some inject first, then untie;

12) Squeeze the cherry the way you would squeeze a nipple to plump it for your eager mouth;

13) Watch the level of liquid: Let the top go all the way into the needle, then quickly pull the blood back up into the barrel;

14) The sauna bursts in your temples, vanishes for a second, then that warm bath works its slow way up your legs, through your crotch, steaming into your neck, up to your head, and finally the warmth nestles like a lover's tongue inside you;

15) If you aren't nodding, pull this wave of warmth in and out, make it sway with you, boot and reboot: push the blood back in, pull it back and.push forth—make it cadent with your heartbeat, make it work like the moon on the tides of your blood and pulse, make it tango with your soul's ebb and flow through that narrow aperture. This is to say, follow steps 4 & 6 with point of needle inside your vein.

So Violet wants a divorce.

"You're a pecker-lapping, donkey-fucking, husband-reaming, bitch-dog," I say and tear her lip open with my fist. A tooth is broken. I shatter our coffee table with a K-Mart folding chair. I rip her blouse. She wears nothing underneath. Ann is screaming in her bedroom. I think I'm really going to get angry when someone decks me from behind.

When I wake up, the apartment is empty. The phone is near my head and it is ringing. My NCO says I have to report to my commander ASAP or I'll be SOL. Violet and Ann have already left for Indiana; she leaves a message saying that she is going to pull out all the calabash in her garden.

In three days, I am flying to California with a refueling in Fairbanks. So the day before I am to be court-martialed in Travis Air Force Base, I call my mother. I want her to fly to California. Maybe she can help me out. On the phone she says, "*Hijo*, wha hoppening to ju?"

"Things are fucked up, Mother. Things are really fucked up for me."

"Gol-LEE wi ju!" she says.

"I know. I know. I know." I have my eyes closed and my head against the stuccoed walls by the phone in the brig. All I can do is roll my head against the wall. "I know. I know."

In no time at all, I am out with a medical discharge. I'm lucky, but my mother cries during the final disposition. She drops her head back and howls with a sadness that transfixes everyone. The judge is visibly shaking, as if my mother's voice is magically thick, magically tangoing with the blood of all of us. When her howl or moan or wail subsides and releases all of us, two black bailiffs take her into the hallway. They handle her gently.

Back in Clowerston, I am put into a halfway center with some nebulous affiliation to Betty Ford's recent outfit. I cold-turkeyed in Okinawa, so this is a detox and counseling. I'm not allowed to speak with anyone outside the center for several days. The idea is that returning to old friends will open the door to old habits. The method seems to be based on a scared-straight psychology. The counselors tell me that I am a wasted human being, flyspeck, less than slug shit. They say that I ought to have more respect for my culture and my race. They say I ought to do something with my fucking life. They say I better get normal or people are going to treat me like hell for the rest of my life—and probably that ain't gonna be too damn long, fool!

I say, "I see what you mean. I sure don't want to do drugs any more. I want to make something of myself. I want to do something so that everyone will be proud that I'm Hispanic."

They ask me to help out in the counseling sessions, be a part of the team effort to set people straight.

"I want to help," I say.

Everyone in the center is white. Except the janitor, that is. In the sessions, everyone calls me Herman.

They like the way I speak when the session is going strong and people are crying because they're so ashamed and they know that what they're feeling is weakness, stupidity or sinfulness. I am able to speak as if I know what it is to be hung up high, impotent, left for public ridicule, yet with the skeletal hope that someday, someone will come to receive this hope and give us a second chance. I speak of waiting for rebirth. I urge them to think positively. I say that no matter what hell we have lost ourselves to, there will come a time when we will be reborn into sunlight. Our lives will once more have the gift of wings. The counselors love the way I speak. Soon, I am allowed to come and go from the center as I please.

My fifteenth time out of the center, I see Violet and Ann getting into a car in front of an IGA grocery store. A man in a purple cape holds the door for them. Ann gets in back. I move to stand in clear sight and when the car passes, Violet gives me the finger. Of course, I try to call Ann the first through the fifteenth time I leave the center, as well as trying every other day from the center, but Violet never passes the phone when I do manage to get an answer.

My mother calls Ann twice a week. "Hey Pancho," she says, and Violet gives the phone to Ann. "How are ju?"

My news of Ann comes from my mother.

"I sink she half an earring probe-blem."

"Oh, Mother, don't tell me that."

"I doe-an sink she speak-ed deh English. She half an earring probe-blem."

"I'm not a good father," I say.

"Pancho, Pancho, Stop-ped dat!"

But no matter how much my mother tells me that it is difficult to be in this country, difficult to be a foreigner, difficult to be a young man in these trying times with so much drugs, I know in my heart that I am simply not a very good father.

"Ease dat guman!" she asserts: "It's that woman," meaning Violet, but Violet, Violet, she's just wanting to find herself. Like me, like everybody, probably.

"I just want to be normal."

My mother spits. "Ack! Why ju wan sohm-thing lie-ked dat? Norm-ol? Is-sed stoopid. Nor-mole. I neber wan be dat. Why, *mijo*, why ju wan-ned dat?" Her eyes are shiny, full of sadness for me, her troubled son. The other children turn out all right, I suppose, but not this son, not this one, not me.

"I'm going to the store, Mother."

At the store, I buy five Polo shirts (one light green, one light blue, one blue-green, one aquamarine, one turquoise), one pair of Docksider shoes, one pair of tartan golf pants, one pair of Islander pants, one pair of Cross Creek pants with front pleats, one pair of Reeboks, and I place an Yves Saint Laurent suit on layaway. At the counter, the young woman rings up the price and is genuinely impressed. She looks deep into my eyes.

"Cash or charge, Mister, uh, Mister, uh . . ." She is fishing with unmistakable body language.

"Sinclair," I finish for her. "Cash."

I have been carrying every penny I own in my pocket since I took up the habit of evading Violet more than two years before. I am not sure exactly how much I have, what with no expenses at the center or at my mother's and with disability plus the pay from Manpower jobs. I know it is near a thousand. I take out the wad in my left pocket and count out five fifties. I unfurl a twenty from the wad in my right pocket. The young woman swirls the tip of her finger around her lips as I get my money in order. I place the bills in her hand and wait for the change.

Her face is flushed. "Baby," she says.

"When do you get off?"

She is all smiles. "With you, Sugar, as many times as you want."

"You party?"

She rips the receipt from the register and tosses her thigh against the drawer to close it. She puts my change into her purse. "Let's go."

"And work?"

"Hey!" she shouts to a man in Customer Service. "I have to go with my brother." She slips her purse strap over her shoulder. "My mother's dying!"

We leave in her car. A beat-up Fiero. Black. She lights a half joint left in the ashtray. My stuff's crammed in back. "Where to?" she asks, holding her toke.

I take the joint from her. "Let's pick something up." I take a hit and wait for her to size me up as to what I'm into. "Whatever you want," I say, my voice squeaking.

"Yeah?"

I let my smoke go.

"Coke?"

"Okay, though I prefer going downstairs."

"Like ludes, you mean?"

"At least."

"Uh-huh," she says.

"You don't have to believe me," I answer.

"You like to fuck?"

I nod and pass her the joint. There're only a couple hits left.

She takes a big hit, stares straight ahead awhile, then smiles over at me. She keeps smiling as she lets the smoke go. "I've never done heroin, or that kinda shit."

"Know anybody who does?"

She looks at me.

"To get some. What do you think?"

"Hey, man, you gotta be careful."

"Well?"

"Sure, I guess. Yeah."

"Cool. Let's get you some white stuff first so we can dance later, but I want some shit for now."

"You got money?"

Now *I* smile. "Baby, I can keep you for weeks," I say.

She reaches out and rubs my thigh, then up to my crotch. She leaves her hand there and feels my erection coming up.

We go into the black part of town and knock at a wood gate between houses. A voice calls out. "Dorothy," the young woman says, and then adds, "And a friend." The voice wants to know who. "Sinclair!" The gate opens and an enormous man looks down at us.

"What's up?"

"He's cool. We just want to shop's all."

The man looks me up and down. He reaches out and gives a quick frisk down my sides and front. Then he sticks his big mitt down my shirt and checks for taps.

"Wallet," he says, hand out.

I give him my wallet, but nothing's in there except an old driver's license and the clinic card.

"Hermanegi—What is this shit?"

"Now you know why they call me Sinclair."

"Money?"

"All we need," I answer.

He jerks his thumb behind him and we go along the side of the house. I feel eyes watching every step. We go up a broken concrete stairway and to a screen door. Dorothy pulls it and taps at the door. A window slide opens, slaps shut and we hear bolts opening. A white man is sitting at a kitchen table. He wears a felt hat with a small red feather on the side. He is dressed well and looks very much out of place, but he is perfectly comfortable, perfectly in control.

He waits for Dorothy to get to the point. The black man who opened the door for us stands behind us.

"Hey, Scot," she says, "you doing okay?" She holds my elbow. "Me and Sinclair were hoping to get a little stuff, you know. Something to play with."

Scot looks carefully at me.

"Look, we just met," I say. I roll up my sleeves to show him the old tracks. None are fresh, but those marks have stayed for a while and I have a couple of knots under the skin where I missed the vein, some abscess scars. "I want some for now, if it's cool. I'll even buy a fit, if you got 'em and I'll do it here."

"What do you want?" His voice is surprisingly high. He's a good-sized man, but his voice is a little high and he speaks with no shred of street in his language. His gestures are small, relaxed, like someone who's never worked to his bones for something only to find failure.

"Two g's of coke, two of H." I pull out money. I don't care how much it is. "And a fit." I know they won't rip me off because it's just too much hassle and I'm going to give them a lot anyway. Besides, Dorothy seems regular enough.

Scot motions for his man to get the stuff. "I will give you a special price," he says. "Six hundred dollars."

I look at Dorothy.

"It's good," she says.

I count out the rest of my money. I have six hundred and seventy-four. In front of him, I empty all my pockets to get every last cent and to show him what I have.

"The syringe is free," he says, maybe thinking I mean to pay more for the fit. "Leave the money here. Dorothy, you two go with Leon."

We enter a family room. The wood floor creaks as we walk across to where Leon holds a bathroom door open. "Knock yusef out," he says, dropping four aluminum wads and a wrapped disposable syringe into my hand. He closes the door behind us.

The bathroom is immaculate. It even has blue fur coverings for the toilet tank and seat cover. The floor has a matching blue rug. The trash can is lined with plastic and the toothbrush holder has a wrapped Reach toothbrush in each of the four holes. I look for a bent spoon in the medicine cabinet, but there isn't one.

"Okay," I say.

Dorothy is antsy with excitement. "I've never fired anything. I've watched lots of times, but I've never done it."

I put the stuff on the toilet tank and hold her face in my hands. We kiss. She opens her mouth and searches for my tongue. She moves to pull back, but I want to kiss more. I nibble her top lip, sucking it just a little, then I nibble her bottom lip. I kiss her until she loosens up. Her muscles relax, and she lets her anxiousness go. I step back.

"I'll do you first."

She sits on the toilet.

I open one of the aluminum packets and hold up the plastic bag inside. The clumps tell me it is coke. The bag is new. I hold my hand under the faucet and suck up four cc of water. Dorothy is watching intently. Her hands stroke my legs beside her. I squeeze out the water into the bag and rub the outside until the coke is dissolved. "Rip off a filter," I say, nodding toward her purse. She gets out a cigarette and pulls off the filter. She takes the opportunity to light one for herself. I make a roll of wadding from an eighth of the filter and push it onto the needle. Then I tip the small bag so that the needle and filter are in the corner and I suck up two cc. A little less. I leave the filter in the bag and zip-lock the top.

I show Dorothy where to press her thumb high under her arm. "Press hard," I say. Her vein is not easy to see, but we wait until pressure builds enough to show a bulge under her skin. I tap it, test the resiliency, figure how deep it is. "Ready?"

Her eyes are sparkling with the danger of it all.

I give her a peck on the lips, then kneel beside her.

She's used to a couple lines at a time because when half the gram hits her heart, she gasps. Her breathing is hard, her eyes flutter and there is a twitch in her neck. This feeling is brand new for her, so she does the only thing she knows which comes close and reaches down with her free hand to touch her crotch the way she might after orgasm: legs pressing together around her fingers, her body squeezing with the exquisite pain. But it is too much. She gags. I lift her and the toilet seat quickly, and push her face down. She vomits once—a thick arc of long stem roses and ballet slippers—and then the pleasure returns. I cup water in my hand and run it around her mouth and neck. Her shirt soaks up the flow.

She wants to kiss, but I hold her back. Really she is hot with her own body, this high, because I prepare myself and she closes her eyes to rub her face cat-like against my stomach. I shoot up my part standing there beside her, hitting the easy veins on the back of my hand. This is almost an old friend—it makes me want to hurry to her house and to the scag. I let the rush pass. Dorothy is trying to work my zipper down.

"Let's go," I say. She is too high, so I pull her to stand up. I gather everything, including her, and we are heading out. No one says anything. Scot doesn't move. Leon heads for the bathroom.

I drive the car following her directions.

She has an apartment overlooking the complex's pool. I close all curtains and turn on a few lights. Dorothy has her clothes off and is stumbling behind me trying to claw my clothes off. We end up in the hallway, on the floor, my knees banging the carpet and getting more raw by the minute. I feel next to nothing. Neither one of us can come. This only makes us fight harder, turn faster, shift to different positions more often. We are both hollering and sweating. She is doing a job with her fingernails and what I want is for all the pain to build high enough, the pain to be realized enough and sharp enough where I can tell myself it is pleasure and then focus it on my cock and finally come. When I do, it feels as if I am gushing blood down there. I am simultaneously screaming and so sure that blood, not semen, is flowing from me that I push Dorothy away and look down. It is only my imagination. Dorothy pulls my face into her crotch so that I can help her finish. She quickly gets impatient and uses her hand instead. When she comes, the plaster cracks and tumbles from the ceiling. We end up covered with dust.

No kidding.

We stay naked. We stay wet. Dorothy brings us a water bottle from the refrigerator and we move into the front room. She punches in a Velvet Underground tape. She straddles me on the couch, facing me, and hooks her arms around my neck. We don't talk. Instead, we sway to the music, and let our hearts catch up to us enough where we might start fucking all over again. It doesn't take long before we are both thinking of maybe hitting again, too. All of this wondering and deciding takes place without a word. We know what the other is thinking by the move of thighs, the rubbing of pelvises, the pressing together of chests, the stirring in me and the hardening of her nipples. Our eyes speak, and our mouths too in nicks and kisses, nipping teeth. And we decide that we'll divide the other gram of coke in four, twice apiece. The rush will be weak, but we can get into each other's bodies more.

"I'll show you a trick to get a better rush," I say.

We do our business on the couch. I assure her that she won't throw up again. Her body won't be going through the same change it did before, I tell her. "Now, your body's asking for more. When you threw up, your body was fighting to keep alive."

This time I have her get a stocking to use as a tie. I fix things up and tell her to release the tie when I say so. This time, I jack it all fast, wait a heartbeat and tell her to untie. As soon as she does, I boot it fast. She feels the second rush. The third boot I do slow so she can see the blood rush back up the barrel and into the small vacuum created by the plunger coming up. I pull the plunger to the top, then shoot it all back. She's out of her mind. That rush is purely psychological. It's the true thrill of shooting. Playing with blood, jacking, on the edge, watching the blood swirl into the barrel. This is what really makes the addict. This is what makes every shooter in the world shoot ice water, alcohol, aspirin, anything soluble. This is what finally makes junkies the demons they become. It is not the drug, it is the blood game, the venal tearing, that makes vampires of addicts.

As soon as I hit my part, we know we will immediately do the rest. As soon as we finish, we plan to do the heroin. Our hearts pound, the smell of intestine, of something deep within the body, is all around us. I know she will die if I give her more than a quarter of a gram. I say, "I'll go first. You take it easy. I'll do you after. Just take it easy. Enjoy the high."

Her teeth are grinding away, her fists tight. "Yeah, okay, sure." She's watching with eyes like a gecko's.

▼

Or at least that's the way I remember her when I wake up. My mother is sitting beside me.

She gets up slowly and stands over me. She has been crying forever. I feel like my mind is somewhere else, like my body is going through one of the worst hangovers known to man, and that I want to say hi to my mother, but my mind can't get close enough to my body to work the gears in my throat and jaw.

My mother lifts her hand high over her head and then it comes crashing against my face. "*Mierda!*" she says, crying hard. "Ju stoopid sheet!"

The slap of her hand hasn't brought my mind closer to my body. I want to say, "What's the matter? Hey, I bought some clothes. Now I can look like those boys I went to school with and get myself a real job. Maybe I can get married to some nice blond woman. Hey, Mother, things are good, things are good, *Mamita*." I know she likes it when I say *mamita*. It works on her the way vaguely familiar scents work on all of us, the way a sound just barely in reach recalls the voices of our distant past.

Apparently, however, I didn't say shit. My mother keeps looking at me as if I'm not quite there. She casts her eyes heavenward as if I'm already gone. You know: dead. Because of that I think that I am off this planet, finally. I see in my mother's face the vision that I have finally crossed over and that I won't have to do any more of this bullshit, play any more of these games with speaking, with feeling, with pretending. The idea is so strong within me that I instantly know what it is to cry with joy. It is sheer weightlessness, that's what it is. The tears come because they float free of the gravity of the body, they float out with the diaspora of the soul journeying to new worlds, uninhabited, uninhibited and free, free, free—free at last!

Once more, I am wrong.

My world is not elsewhere, out there, in distant climes. My world is straight in front of me and entirely through my eyes. Most often, the world is the one thousand, five hundred and twenty four holes in the ceiling tile above my hospital bed. When my mother comes to visit, my world gets propped at an angle because of pillows, but comes to rest straight in front. Sometimes it is side to side, if my mother moves my head to show me something with real width or real depth.

The second day I am awake, she kneels by the bed and drapes her arms over my body and cries. When she has wrung herself dry, she stands up and says, "Ju lissen to me, Pancho. I doe-an wan ju be de stoopid modder fackor any more. An if ju die dis time, Pancho, I am dying *tambien*. We die togedder, ju hear? I am fighding bode me an ju. An ju know what, Pancho?—I am a berry good modder! Ju gwill see!"

The third day I am awake, Mother brings me posters from Guatemala and hangs them all around the room. She puts a sheet over my face and straddles my head with her feet to staple a poster over the ceiling tile. She climbs down and removes the veil from my face. I look into a strange painting of a seated woman, hand held up to a tree which holds a biting skull. Everything is red and blurred, the woman's head is tiny, triangular, the body jointed like a mannequin's body, the style is expressionistic. In the upper right corner is the name Roberto González Goyri. I don't know what any of this is.

My mother stands beside me. We both look up at the poster. Then one corner pulls loose and flaps down.

"*Puchis*," she says, and covers my face again to restaple the thing. I don't know what that is either. My mother is just as liable to say things in Spanish that are purely Guatemalan as purely idiosyncratic and invented.

The fourth day I am awake, I wait for my mother and stare at the poster. Okay, I think, obviously I am the skull and my mother is the seated woman reaching out to me. Simple enough.

That same day, my mother props me up and Ann comes into view. My mother moves my head from side to side. No one else is in the room. Ann is standing by the door, which opens shortly after my mother lets go of my head.

Ann is beautiful. She seems tall for a seven year old. She keeps staring at me. It allows me to really see her, though. Her skin is dark with Hispanic blood. Her hair has my blackness, and is straight like mine. She has the thick lips and broad face of the ladino, much more than I do. She looks more Guatemalan than I do. Pretty. Dark. Modest. Carrying everything with comfort that I have fought against. Her skin is the color of pecan nuts. Smooth. And there is something shiny at the top of her pupils. It is difficult to see, and disappears in her brown eyes when I try to focus on it. But it is shiny, pregnant with light, I think. Her eyes have small blossoms of twin lights.

I am so ashamed that I want Ann to leave. I cannot move my head and when I close my eyes to keep this angel from humiliating me, her sheer beauty, her distant calmness, forces my lids open and, once more, I am engulfed by deep shame.

Then when she says, "Daddy," something snaps inside my heart. I believe for a moment that I am hemorrhaging, there is such a flood inside of me, and the pain in my body is excruciating, so excruciating that I know I am screaming. Suddenly, I understand that my mind has come back, it has returned to my body, and that my body is a coil of shattered pieces each screaming out in its own anguish, each begging for relief. I understand that my mind has dropped from wherever it had leaped to protect itself from the physical and is now tossing on the horrid swells of this boiling sea of pain that is my body.

My mother comes back with Ann and a doctor and two nurses, and all of them chatter around me, poke and stick me. The pain subsides into an approaching dream of sleep. In the shadows of that approaching fog, Ann touches my hand and says, "Daddy, oh Daddy, please don't die."

On the fifth day I am awake, I am awake for the first time. I can move my head and the words I use are audible, though not pronounced particularly well. My mother and I can hold a type of conversation. I learn that I was in a coma for two months. My mother says it is a miracle that I am alive. Evidently, Dorothy called the ambulance and is all right. Mother says that I will be allowed to go home soon. She does all she can to *not* say that I will never be the same, but I know. Most of my words come out of saliva bubbles that pop on my chin.

The sixth day I am awake, Mother tells me that I look good with a beard. She tells me that Violet has moved to New York with her husband. She tells me that Violet promises to bring Ann once a year to see me until I can manage to see her on my own; then I can visit as much as I like. Mother tells me that *she* has started to do sculptures again and that the house is full of them. I tell her that my mind is exactly the same as it ever was, it's just my body that's in bad shape, like I can't remember what "mouth" or "face" is.

"*Jesú' Chorizo*," she says. That's it: Jesus Sausage. That's what she says when I try to tell her that I'm okay inside.

The seventh day I am awake, the doctors run a battery of tests on me. Mother doesn't see me all day. I hear her once down a hallway, shouting in Spanish that a mother has a right to see her ailing son. Evidently she doesn't.

And two days after that I am in a wheelchair and in my mother's house. I can control my arms and fingers pretty well. My legs are funky. My mother has things all over the house that she wants me to see. In one room there is a strange sculpture made of cement. The rectangular shape has legs and arms and the backs of heads. But overpowering all of it is a huge vagina with clitoris and labia and everything. On the underside, the vagina is a flower blooming out of the contorted and entwined human limbs. Another work has a giant bird giving birth to an even larger egg. The poor creature is broken on the ground, its wings flapping in pain, its legs trying to lift from its open vulva an enormous and broken egg. The hatchling is nowhere to be seen. The bird struggles in its private agony, fighting this injustice of life that makes birthing such a beautiful torture.

Elsewhere are odd configurations of wood shapes, animals with human features who struggle to break free of either their human side or of their animal side, and dozens of abstract entities in combat with definite forms. Creatures with blowguns, half human, half planets, fighting against indescribable beasts.

Mother is girlishly excited: "How ju like it, *mijo*? Dese are my Espanish for ju. Dese are jour Espanish."

"I don't know what to say."

"Ju bedder know. Dese say-bed jour life."

"What?"

"I were-ked dese so ju can sur-bibe."

"What are you talking about?"

"Dese are de tings I were-ked from de tings dat were in ju for so many jears. Like any-mals. Day are de libes enside ju. I take en my berry hands de debils dat I fine-ed ober jour bawdy an den I come home to may-ked dese tings."

I kiss her on the cheek. I think she's a nutbar, but I kiss her on the cheek. "Thanks, Mother."

"Doe-an ju tell nobody," she says.

"I swear to God, Mother. I won't ever tell anyone the truth."

She goes upstairs and leaves me to push my way around at my leisure. All I can do is look at her stuff. It's everywhere. Everything is struggle. Everything is a fight. The love that I do find—shiny disks, iridescent wings, crystal—is all embedded in rough clay, dark colors, layers and layers of guises, like Hindu maya over her magic-realist characters. And one work is really a series of works, starting with an amorphous lump of clay spotted with flecks of light, swatches of cloth, and bric-a-brac. The next begins to have appendages, the light comes from pieces of gold-plated jewelry, the cloth rising out of the clay. And each piece has finer detail, each moving toward a hominid, each sculpted as if moving forward, reaching out. And most are trailing vestiges of first fish, then amphibians, then mammalians, all the way to the third from last which has primate aspects. The next to last is very much like the first amorphous lump yet without anything embedded in it. The last is partly hominid—the chest and up—but the bottom part looks at first like just randomly scratched clay. It isn't until I look closer that I see that the legs and part of the belly are composed of various figures blending into one another. I can distinguish parrots, alligators, monsters, crowds of boys, storm clouds, the Guatemalan flag, corpses, a calabash like a soccer ball among ghastly players, two boys with heads like the sun and moon.

And although I understand none of this, all of it disturbs me. My mother wants me to believe her sculptures are the manifestations of my demons. Fine. My mother wants me to know that this series is my life in ways more genuine, more true, than could ever be in mere representation. These are her Espanish, she said. These are my Espanish.

I think she really believes in magic. So be it. I think she saved my life, somehow, and that it's my duty to set myself right by her. And for Ann, working her way up dark northern streets to find her own way into sunlight. In fact, I am so full of this as an end to what I was that I go toward the bathroom, without giving it a second thought, when I stop and say to myself, "How the hell am I going to do this?" And it means much more than using the bathroom. I'm at no end at all. *Jesú' Chorizo*, this is just the barest beginning. And that scares shit out of me. I mean, will Ann grow to love me? Will I ever get to a point where I will not shame my mother? Will I ever set things right? Did I really have twins from my little and inconsequential spitting? And why twins? And what, sweet Lord, might they have become?

I TELL YOU THIS

I HAVE BEEN AWAKE FOR HOURS. ANNIE HAS just curled up behind me. The hairs of her pussy are nestled between my cheeks. Perhaps in her sleep she has forgotten that we went to bed angry, hating, swearing this would be the end, our thing together. Perhaps the sleep seeping through her has made her forget who she's in bed with.

The walls are slashed with light from the Venetian blinds and the streetlamp on the corner. Her Indian batiks are dark, indistinguishable in night except for the longer light bands streaking one. Once more, it is the cut of the street in our lives. The cut of street. Light now that is razoring through our windows, our blinds that should be stopping any bit of New York from creeping in.

I have said the place is seedy. Everything in New York is seedy. Even the best here is somehow outgrowth from the compost around it. I try not to think of our fight.

Instead, I listen to the plastic cup turning outside. The window is open because the radiator is too hot. It is cold as infidelity outside. Cold as a single goldfish, cold as the Saharan night.

We are on the fifth floor, yet from the street in front, we seem to be on the first. The second floor, if you count street-level as one. It is because we live on Haven in the upperwest side. The lower floors descend into the cliff below and behind us to overlook the Hudson River, the George Washington Bridge and the twin nightmares of Riverside Drive and Henry Hudson Parkway. The plastic cup in the street is loud because it is late.

We live at the joint of a "T." 173rd is straight in front. Haven curves south to become 168th and north to a ramp for the Henry Hudson P. Whether because of the 'T' of Haven or because of the park like a plateau on one side and the straight-faced tenements on the other, the plastic cup is merely circling in the street. I know it will circle for days. The trash outside never really moves, it only circles in little whirlwinds or larger whirlwinds that may seem to the unaware or to those agog at surfaces as if there is real movement, but none of it really moves.

I have watched trash for days from my window because I cannot write these days. I watched a manila envelope, an SASE—is it "an" SASE or is it "a" SASE?: Now you see why I cannot write; it is the difference between the rules of the written and the rules of the spoken, how something sounds and how something is supposed to be. Christ! It is self-indulgence.

So I watched it swirl on the street for ten days until it was accidentally swallowed by the streetsweeper. On Monday and Thursday the cars on this side double park on the other side for the sweeper. On Tuesday and Friday the other side double parks on this side. The sweepers push the garbage from one side to the other. I have learned to get up from my desk whenever I hear the machines come because I want to see which pieces of trash will happen to be pulled into the brushes of the machines. I have learned to guess correctly. It all depends on where they are in the whirlwind when the cars are moved or not really moved, depending on your breadth of vision. The shift in currents alters the tiny maelstrom and then the sweeper machine comes whirring on. This is how the SASE is eaten. Yet the plastic cup swirls still. It is surviving the same way a fly survives between panes of glass.

I try to imagine its path. Annie mewls against me like a cat. Her translucent blond hairs tickle me. Her breasts are warm. Her breath smells bad. The leaves have fallen for days and they too enter the circuit outside. I can imagine the leaves from the park, mostly yellow and orange-red elm leaves now, the newspaper that a passer-by dropped two days ago, the plastic cup that appeared one day while I was deep in thought and oblivious to the noise sweeping up from the street, and the bags and paper that are shit-stained because dog owners pick up their pets' droppings only to drop them surreptitiously a few feet away. It is 4:30 in the goddamned morning.

I do not want to recall our argument. I do not want to think about the plastic cup. I do not want to see how the street light is appropriately cutting through our window. I remember instead the story I read in my new journal before Annie came home and we had our marathon fight. It is really cold in here. It is a mistake to leave the window open even that little bit. I told her. Closed it is hot, but hot is better than cold. I am from Florida. Annie is from Chicago. You see. It is fall and I do not know if I will be able to take winter in New York. Atlanta is too cold for me. New York is what?—freezing and filthy! It is freezing, filthy and a fucking mess. It makes people like itself. All of this is part of the argument that I do not want to think about. I do not want to think about it.

Whatever happened to the garbage barge we heard so much about? Is there some man piloting it still? Is his face and body disintegrating because of the fumes from that tonnage of NYC refuse? Is the barge circling forever the seven seas? Is this by someone's order, circling, until all of it just decomposes; atom upon atom lifting away into the air, each to become a single neural tick in someone's respiratory system?

I've looked over the walls along the walkway between our apartment building and the ramp to the drives below. I have seen barges moving up and down the Hudson. From the top of our building I can see a sewage treatment plant on the river. Once, I walked down the walking bridge by our building and down to Riverside Park. I discovered an entire community of street people living under the overpasses and the bridges and cloverleaves that make up the Washington Bridge, Henry Hudson P. and Riverside Drive. One woman even had a bed and dresser against an embankment. Several fires were going. People were just eating their meals from cans, smoking dope and drinking. For the most part they didn't give a shit about me. Some asked me for a cigarette. At the bottom, in the median between the walkway of Haven Cliffs and the park, dozens of wrecked and stripped cars served as shelters. In the park more cars had been left. The wrecks were ravaged so that only the most useless of wires and hardware was left. By the Hudson River, car seats littered the rock banks as if people used them to leisurely take in the splendor of this grimy river lapping Manhattan.

There is human shit everywhere. There are clear markings where a person has made a temporary home. I have come to recognize them. The distinguishing marks are easy: a plastic bag of clothes, nearby a campfire made of broken cinderblock, a rusty hibachi, scrapmetal from a car or major appliance, and empty cans of Vienna sausage, pork and beans, chili-dog mix, dog food. There is a bottle somewhere close by. Sometimes a bag of empty aluminums, some glass and plastic bottles, large ones. When I see bags of cans left I know that something awful has happened because they would not have left these by choice. These things are money.

I do not like this train of thought either. I do not like much of anything anymore. I did not want to come to New York. I do not want to stay. Annie is making her way into things here, but I am not. My writing is not going well. I lean against the windowsill and watch the happenings far too much. I see the trash swirl; she moves in and out of it.

I think maybe I should get up and close the window because it is really cold outside. My whole body feels like it's shriveling. The cup swirls. The sound of leaves whirling. I get up and close the window.

I look at the cover of the journal by my feeble notes. The first story is terrible. It is first person present tense and I hate it. Like purple or spiked hair, first person present tense is the face of things. I write in past tense. I hate the story because I know that today everything is on the surface. Everything that matters is just on the face of things. This is what postmodernism is. Fiction in journals swirls like the trash outside, only seeming to move and change, when it does not. And I know that this is what I must do or I will just have to set up my own hibachi, hunt for aluminum fiction to sell to journals, find a stoop to sleep near.

But this is just another diversion because really it is the fight that has brought me to this point and not the writing. The fight may draw these things too. Yet it is not the state of literature, but the fact that New York City is the filthiest place I have ever lived in, including places all over the goddamned world. And it is looking to be colder than betrayal, colder than stupidity in power, colder than having to give in, than the plethora of M.F.A. editors of literary journals. What do they know of anything?

Right here I crumple this story. Because present tense is something beyond sense, I can say that I take this story and crumple it. Yes this one. I crumple this very story. I despise what I am doing. I think I will rip the pages apart but I do not. I think about it for some time more and I think without using contractions in my language because that too is part of it all. And instead I throw the paper into the trash can. I bend down and swirl the papers I have dropped. A comma is the furthest thing from my mind. This is vestige. This is indulgence.

Back in bed it is warmer. I feel Annie's pussy hair against my buttocks and know that we are nearing the end. Maybe this is what is happening to us. This swirling. I feel the cold again and put my hand between my legs. My hand curls around my penis because I am still so cold. The head of my penis is cold. My penis is shriveled because of the cold. It feels like a chicken heart taken from a thawing bird. It feels so small. I wonder how it could ever make anyone happy, it is so small. I remember something that says that men's penises are getting larger. Perhaps evolution is doing this. Women are choosing large penises more and more and so the smaller penises are becoming maladaptive. Culled out, evolutionarily speaking. The large penis is adaptive. The large penis is breeding more and perpetuating itself. Who can blame a woman for dumping a small penis? The fittest survive in nature's order. Are vaginas enlarging—or would that be maladaptive? No, it is the inverse relationship that is being perpetuated. The little penis in my hand gets colder and smaller. I am convinced that what I have between my legs is nothing more than a chicken neck with a chicken heart attached to it. Under them there is a cold and tiny octopus sac. How could anyone like what I have here?

I would be better if I were a woman and Annie my husband. Would I be able to take misfortune better? Would my sorrow be something easily petted away by my husband? Would I be absolved of guilt and anything I did be acceptable because of the tyranny of men, the liberation of women, the confines of everything? Would infidelity never be my fault? Would betrayal be a sharp bone to merely pluck from my mouth and place on the rim of the plate?

I think I am a woman and Annie is my husband:

I am like we are now, but instead of hair I feel her thick and flaccid penis lolling against my buttocks. In the morning, when we are stirring from sleep I stretch and yawn. My cheeks press against her and her penis slowly unfurls, fills and looms against my buttocks and lower back. She has a very large penis. I did not marry her because of it, but I am glad that she does. Her arm drops around me, gathers up my breasts and she hugs me. I feel her lips kissing against my cheek, searching in the morning laziness for my mouth. She is being lazy, half asleep. I shift and the length of her penis plops between my legs so that I can feel it lightly rub both my pussy and my anus. It feels wonderful. I know that she loves me. She doesn't say it much, but she is always rubbing my ass, petting me and kissing my neck when we are alone. We have been fighting but yesterday she said that my needs really did matter. She said she loved me. So today I allow her to do something that she likes. I raise up so she can move closer. The head of her penis slowly pushes against my anus, bending the muscle in. I feel her pressing forward and the heaviness slides gently into my pussy from behind. It hurts a little because she is so big. Huge. But I get used to it fast because I can feel her pleasure just in the sounds coming from her mouth. Her pleasure is important to me. Her arms feel light around me, full of a genuine satisfaction because I have allowed her to do this. She begins rocking. Her penis reaches far up inside me, so that my breath is gone. Annie turns my face with the flat of her hand so that our lips join. She does not move fast or hard, but I know she is enjoying how tight it feels around her and how I am completely soft for her. Receptive. She does not want to hurt me. It is only something she likes, wants to try like anal sex.

Because of this scene, I get up from bed and go to the trash can. I take out this story from among the newspaper and junk and unfold the pages for you. You.

At the end of the story there is another whirlwind. The flurry is not unlike Dorothy's Kansas storm. I can see inside it. I tell you there are people whirling about inside it. There are hibachis and plastic coffee cups and chickens and penises, large and small, and *The Iowa Review* and bombed out cars with AIDS-bitten-drug-addicted-mentally-unstable streetpeople and the *AWP Newsletter*, the word "grammar," and Annie rolling like a hoopsnake so that her enormously long penis wraps around her back and enters her mouth. All of these things are at the end, in the end of this story that I uncrumple from the trash. All these things are in this final paragraph, this vertiginous whorl that finally stops at a very curious "you."

WOMAN OF THE BUS

BECAUSE OF HER I HAVE GIVEN UP ON THE 1 train and even the A. I ride the 4 bus now from Washington Heights to the 104 and down to 5th Ave. It is slow slow yet I have watched that woman ride the bus. I have seen her turn, Chekhovian, one supple calf raised, her ankle a sudden blossom of lines, her hand curving brilliantly around the rail. Bright silver railings, catching light. You see the flash that is forever burned into nous. So I have given up on the infernally bad 1. I let loose the blessed A. Watch her skirt just behind her knees. Wish my mouth at that juncture.

She ascends at any of several stops near Columbia-Presbyterian. Me: the Cloisters. The weather can be anything at all, it doesn't matter. Birds; exact clothes? Name them yourself. For I have seen that woman of the bus. I have descended as early as the George Washington Bridge to run along Ft. Washington in hopes of watching her climb the steel stairs, snap open her purse and toy with that coin eater. I have stood close enough to smell the sweat of her toil way uptown. It is a hyacinth on her shoulder. I have grazed my forearm to help her lift a bundle to the overhead. And in her quick crossing of legs, I have seen an obsidian sea that mocked the white stars above and suspended a moon neither sea nor star but blue and frightened like me.

"Woman of the bus, I have watched you."

"Get the fuck away from me."

She stares from the window, her palm inches from the glass so that in the evening reflection it is her eyes I see full of privacy. I wish the tip of my tongue within her life-lines, between her ammoniated fingers.

"I wish your tired hands would work just a little more with me."

"Creep!"

By now all the women are staring, the men with warning eyes. She shifts away and her sleeveless blouse opens beneath her arm.

"There is the hint of islands."

She moves to a farther seat. A large black man standing by the rear exit turns sideways in the aisle to block me from moving near her.

"Wait! Please! I have come here and wished I could rest my face in your hands. I know the very dirt you work in! I watch you look out over the city. You have sad eyes. You have crows in your head that fly out over everything. God, I've wanted you to dip your hands into my belly and let your blackness run like ink into my veins. Don't you see? I want you to dye my moon-flesh, you to love me."

The black man peers at her. The women peer at me.

She jabs her finger against the black band so the driver will stop.

"I have pale eyes for you!"

This time there is nothing I want that happens. Oh, perhaps a shattering of ice, the tiniest of chips from some granite wall.

"Don't worry yourself for the woman."

"I have pale eyes for her."

The man looks down at his feet as I leave the bus. He moves a little so that I think he will console my shoulder, but he does not.

I do not go on the bus for two days. For two days I eat nothing but purple onions purchased from a Dominican man by St. Nicholas and 165th. I pass him after I mail a letter addressed simply to "Woman Of The Bus; #4; NYC 10032." It costs me $0.87 because I use a 6x9, No. 55 envelope with metal clasp and there are five heavy sheets of paper folded in half. I write a sentence on each sheet:

"Your arms hold a continent of dreams."

"Coconuts surround the world, ignoring the barriers of water, of land, of strife."

"The buttons of your blouse belong in my mouth."

"You might have turned me to ash."

"You might have turned me to ash."

My stomach enters into battle with me and I give up the onions. I eat two bunches of cilantro, chopped and spread among all the slices of a loaf of Wonderbread and go to sleep. In the morning I run in Fort Tyron Park so that my bowels will move. I eat a good lunch of Ethiopian *full* at the Red Sea on 125th and Broadway, under the shadow of the elevated 1 track. I pick up the 4 and will ride it until she appears if it takes all of eternity. I don't care.

When she appears I get on my knees in the aisle.

"For two days I have thought only of you. My head is completely filled with the horizons of your evenings."

"Boy, you the biggest fool. Why you come to me like this? Why?"

I take off my shirt so that she can see the answer in my flesh. I take off my pants, my shoes and socks. I take off my underwear.

"The poor chi-el in love."

"He a damn fool."

The other women shake their heads. They come closer to me.

"He love you."

She turns away and presses her dark face against the oily windowpane.

"Don't you know I do nothing but work? I ain't got time for playing no games."

One of the women has no teeth. She guides me from my knees and makes me sit on the edge of the seat. Her hands are like cherry root. She cradles my scrotum, measuring. The other women surround me.

"Why he doing this? Why?"

"He helpless. He poor and in love. He like a boat gone way away from home, now."

The toothless woman squeezes my dickhead so that the blood swells in the capillaries. She measures the length of my erection by using the old dents in her gums. She wiggles her hands side to side as if to say, well, it's not bad. Then she opens her mouth wide so she can use it to measure the girth of my testicles.

"He okay underneath."

"He love you, girl."

She looks at me now. The other women urge her to smile at me. My heart is beating so fast that my erection falls. A different woman reaches down and inserts her finger into my rectum. She teases my prostate so the blood comes back.

"Look how he love you."

Toothless pinches Woman Of The Bus hard above the elbow.

"You take him home. No more a this stuff."

All of them guide her to me. I get back down on my knees. I slowly press my face into her crotch. Even through the skirt I can smell the perfume of hurricanes, of mountains. I cannot help myself. I begin to cry.

"Okay."

As I leave, the driver gives me my transfer.

"Thank you."

Everything is black. Our perspiration. Our breath. The heat from our bodies. The friction between us. So that I cry again and she takes me up with her arms and kisses each of my eyes.

"You making one hell of a burden on me."

I can hardly speak because of my crying.

"It's really you."

"Sure, ah-hum. Never mind. We see."

Woman Of The Bus leans back on the bed and opens her thighs again. This time I go in all the way until I am safely positioned inside her womb. Her legs close over me and all the light is gone. Black the amniotic sea. Black the heartbeat of my mother. Black the umbilicus now, crackling with something no white woman can ever possess. No stars here, no frightened moon. Only the rocking of ancient waters. Only the tides of life slapping ships burdened with dark cargo. Around me the clattering of metal links. Something old trying to deny itself. Something of betrayal and shame.

Inside her I feed on the ancestry of lions, the heritage of antelope. Always I hear the drumming of ships. The panther of her lungs purrs into me. Her claws scratch slowly the membranes of my ears, her blood delicious in my mouth, so that I do not ever want to leave the black warmth of her womb.

But she, riding the bus, breaks water and licks me clean. In her breasts again, I suckle from her tamarind nipples a fountain of marrow.

"Burden, like I say."

"No."

"What you want?"

"I want all women to be black as my wife."

"Wife!"

"I want them all to be night travelers."

"Boy, I done took the stars from your life and that sad little moon you was and now you want me to dip into the whole blessed world, too? Burden!"

I shake my head.

"You got legs, don't you."

"Please. Don't make me go."

"It's got to be this way."

She holds me and licks my hair until it is soaked and flat against my skull.

"You still white."

"Please."

I try to catch the eyes of the other women on the bus, but they all turn away. Even Toothless.

"I love you."

"You loves truth. An decency, I gives you that, but I never be your wife. If I anything I be your mama."

The other women nod when I look at them. Toothless stands up. She is old old.

"Go on now."

"It's got to be."

I take out my penis for them, but they shake their heads.

Toothless says, "Time be done for that, boy. Go on use it uptown an downtown so's you do your mama proud. But don't you be shaking it here. A boy ain't a man till he leave home."

"Come here."

I move to her.

Woman Of The Bus kisses me on the forehead. Her heart is oil, covering me, seeping into my pores to drench the insides of my body.

"Warrior. Black warrior," she whispers.

Toothless nods beside her.

"Your weapon be that shallow white skin."

"Yeah? Where I go?"

Toothless smiles. "Now you be right."

"Live on an fight," Woman of the Bus says. "Be a guerrilla."

She gives me the power sign.

"Yeah," I say. "Okay."

CROSSING THE BORDER

SHELL AND BONE

THE WAVES HAD BEEN PUSHING UP SHELL AND bone for many years, and always—as I lifted the small and brittle pieces, pressing them against my cheek, or carefully turning and maneuvering the smallest ones so they would lie couched and secretive in my ears, or pursing my lips to let the long thin shells rest against my nostrils like some foreign mustache—the mere coloring of these pieces shouted Guatemala.

It did not matter that I was living in Indiana, far from any salt swept automobile paint. And it did not matter, either, that my family had previously lived in Michigan, again far from any imposing waves. The shell and bone came wherever I lived. Often I awakened, my room inundated by the myriad forms of brittle calcium—amassed during the night as if by dreams.

I can't say that it usually annoyed me. When I was bothered by the constant trail of salt smell it was because in Indiana, in Michigan, one is trailed by other things. It would be far different to be bumping incessantly into red-crossed cloth, finely wrought coins, or any number of other things. But shell and bone of the sea—no! It didn't often bother me because friends were friends and the adults lived on the edge. On the contrary, as I got older, the increase of shell and bone came accompanied by a quickened breath, a growing pride, and a marrow-deep curiosity.

My parents never spoke of the shells that flowed freely from my pockets. They acted as if the bone didn't exist, and became expert at changing the direction of my questions. Often, they tried to cement me to tasks at hand.

There were no long hours of sweeping millions of intricately shaped objects from my room in the mornings. The act was illusion. My mother never grumbled over her chin while dumping each of my drawers onto the floor to whisk away the shell. My father would always sit at his desk, writing and thinking, and absently brush away the bone. He would sit, painfully, on a large abalone or place a broken arm of a starfish into his mouth like a pencil.

Once, I gathered food and other provisions to last two months—not forgetting my large pillow with seascape embroidery and waited on his desk for an irrefutable sign of recognition. At first, I would confront him each time he bumped uncomfortably into one of my shells, but my voice must have become too weak. By the end of one month, my interest shifted more and more to the baseball games outside. There were fewer and fewer shells, anyway.

By the end of each summer, the shell and bone returned with a vengeance. One year, my school took up the study of history and geography. One day, as I walked back from my small school, wishing I were older and able to take driver's education, I was struck by the number of workmen encircling the house. They were repairing the windows and doors. Shells covered the yard. More shells than I had ever seen. *Guatemala*. Suddenly, like the flight of cavern bats, a torrent of calcium blew up from the chimney. An especially polite workman told me not to worry about it. Inside, my father spoke to the principal, arranging by phone my transfer into another course. Thereafter, I studied the history of Afghanistan, leaving Central America behind. My mother's shoulders sagged wearily, silently.

You can imagine, then, how I felt when my father came to me and said that the two of us would be going to Guatemala.

That night, in my room, I turned the shell and bone in my hands and watched it pour from my closet. I wished that there would be a plan to it all, but I was raised to believe differently. The idea that shell and bone actually followed me through the streets, built up by my bed and flowed like the Colorado River because of a grand design fascinated me. I wanted to believe that, partly.

On the other hand, the shell and bone had to follow the laws of knowledge: that each fact is a portion of a large, all-encompassing body of laws— regardless of the area the fact comes from. All facts must coexist. No single one can contradict another. But to say that this is by design is another thing. It is inevitable.

Days before we left, I turned the pieces in my hand. To my surprise, two pieces sided up to each other as if broken from a larger piece. For the first time, I examined them carefully. There are small and delicate symbols etched into them. I noticed then, too, that the pieces have a darker side. It was so obvious that I wonder now why I had never noticed. I cleared a circle and turned hundreds of pieces onto their dark side, leaving the white and etched side exposed.

It was foolish to think that I would find more pieces that fit together. There had been countless billions swept away already. However, as if to support my theory about them, I did notice that some of the markings and shapes seemed to be separated within the larger puzzle by only a few pieces. Others seemed so dissimilar as to be separated by hundreds of thousands of shell and bone. I made more room, building up the calcium against my four walls, but only the first two pieces fit together. I fell asleep, wanting desperately to have the shell and bone connect.

The next day, my mother touched me, motioned for me to sit. She was glad that I would finally visit Guatemala. They had waited too long already to show me where I was born.

My father spoke very little. "Marco," he said, "we left when you were three years old."

My mother said that duty demanded I see my father's father, the infamous Ezíqiuel. The *infamous* Ezíqiuel. He was the eldest of the family. He knew the shells, I was sure of it! The thought struck me with the same intensity as finding the two adjoining pieces—no! Some things are too melodramatic.

We left unceremoniously.

The capital of Guatemala is like so many other cities: with factories, noise, ugliness and stink. My father borrowed a car to make the trip into the countryside where Ezíquiel lived. The road became dirt a hundred miles from the village, then narrow horse trails several miles away. We walked.

I can never know what my father feels. I can only surmise that he feels very little which he will show. It's a miracle to me that my legs did not erode on that long walk, so that when we finally arrived, I would be nothing but teeth scurrying to carry my nose, eyes and forehead. The dryness saved me from that intolerable boredom: One needs moisture to dissolve.

Cattle grazed in the fields far off, and men on horseback rode the distant hills. The only life close to us was that of insects, birds and lizards. *There* was a tight chain: The birds ate lizards, the lizards ate insects, and the insects sucked the blood and skin from beneath the oily feathers. All this within coil after coil of cacti.

"About three hundred people live here," my father said.

His voice shocked me. I looked at his face, but he plodded on.

It was an amorphous village and yet the cacti obeyed some instinctual boundary no matter how spread out the houses were. Empty red earth lay between the cacti and the first fruit-laden trees of the village. The bare strip was no more than thirteen feet wide—a fat border of ground. I noticed the various fruit trees: banana, mango, coconut, lime, pineapple, and others I didn't know. Just like people, pigs, chickens and donkeys roamed the main street. The notion that I was so directly related to animals pleased me, but I knew it was pure fantasy. These were the domestic animals of real people.

"The village is very poor. No food. No medicine."

It annoyed me that he spoke so abruptly, without warning. The annoyance sharpened my vision and I saw that his quietness was due to his reading. I could only assume that he had been reading the entire time, as usual. I read the long title: *Meta-phenomenology*.

Just then, I stepped into a large and smelly pile of pig manure. I used a stick to scrape it off, but instead the stuff spread upwards. The odor was terrible. In exasperation, I looked to my father for help. He was also smeared with shit. He removed a handkerchief from his pocket and made two small cones in the cloth. Very carefully, he stuffed each cone into a nostril. He remained expressionless through the entire procedure. His back straightened, and he held his head higher, but the cloth hid his mouth.

Before I could comment, villagers came running with shouts of welcome. They were covered with dung also, but against their hard brown bodies the smell was tolerable. They smiled abundantly, never missing an opportunity to show their broad yellow teeth. They spoke rapidly and chaotically as we were guided through the village. We walked to the square, where we were given fruits as tokens of welcome. My father lifted his veil to bite, then let the cloth drop. Children danced and chattered around us like a great flurry of chickens. The activity made me forget my dung-covered legs, and I hugged even the most besmeared villager. These were my people—my heritage!

A shout arose as a woman, laughing raucously, broke through the clearing atop an enormous pig. Both were covered with slime. A cheer exploded from the people. Several children threw themselves into mud holes and squirmed about happily. One heavy man pushed bananas into his mouth until the pulpy material dripped from his nose and ears like ground beef. He vomited and laughed, his belly bouncing against his thighs.

I asked my father when we would see Ezíquiel and he said later, not here. The villagers never stopped laughing and dancing about.

At night, a marimba played while children accompanied with reed flutes. We feasted on a tremendous meal of refried beans and tortillas placed on huge clay platters. My father gave me a salty cheese to try. Using a tightly rolled tortilla, I drank fruit juices from deep orange gourds. Several women danced and sang to the marimba.

It wasn't until I had nearly finished this bean-filled meal that I saw the manufacture of shell. On the downbeat of their dance, the women threw back their facess and let bits of shell and bone drop from their mouths. I sat, fascinated by the musical timing of the clattering pieces. The bone clicked along with the wooden marimba.

I leaped to my feet with questions, but they told me nothing about the shell. I would find out tomorrow, they said. Only Ezíquiel can tell you of the shell and bone, they said.

I slept in a hammock between a house and a tree. During the night, I frightened away two pigs that came to nibble my toes. "I love it here," I thought to myself. Here is where the shell came from. My grandfather was the man of shell and bone! That was what I thought then.

We proceeded through and out of the village at sunrise, opposite the end we entered. The cacti returned immediately after the red strip. Just the two of us walked down the steep cliff to where the Motagua flowed like chocolate. The sheer hills were half concealed with vines that swept down from the flatland above. An iguana scampered up the gray rock and disappeared over a crest.

I could hear what sounded like a great cascading of water beyond the wall of granite, but when we made the bend I saw no waterfall. Instead, dozens of people busily filled boxes and bags with my shell and bone. Here was where the bone flowed! It was a factory of shellmen, an industry of boneworkers. They never stopped, even when I tried to speak with them. A single woman communicated to us, but it was only to raise her arm and point down the river. My father nodded.

"Cousins," he said to me.

Then, his abruptness didn't bother me. I was glad he'd spoken. It reassured me. Nervously, though, I held his sleeve and realized what a rare person he was to have come from a place like this. His silence made sense then. He had too much to say and, therefore, couldn't say anything. The mere fact that he could read incomprehensible books while these people couldn't read at all, impressed me. To save his mind, however, he had forfeited his mouth.

We turned again along the serpentine Motagua and spotted my grandfather's hut sitting some hundred feet from the bank. I had plenty of time to see: low sweeping ground from the hut, beaten hard under the feet of women going for water or taking clothes to pound on the wet flat rocks.

And from where we walked, the two-room hut seemed empty of people. The walls were made of branches lashed together with vines. An adobe wall could be seen through the gaps in the external walls. The roof was a lattice of palm and banana leaves. A narrow gate, hinged with leather thongs, opened the branch fence encircling the house. And inside the small corral, pigs groveled, chickens scurried and an emaciated dog lay stiffly beside a cactus. As we neared, the dog rose and barked, his short hair rising weakly on his spine. My father hissed. The dog backed away, then watched us enter the fenced area.

The leather thongs rubbed the wood brace and stroked a long chord like the sea-wasp pleading for the eye of the nautilus. The animals stayed away, watching us with their small eyes.

I trembled. Looking back now, I see very clearly that I trembled. I wouldn't now. Not now.

As soon as we entered the hut, we were confronted with an overpowering smell of urine. I spit to remove the smell from my mouth. My father still had his nostrils plugged. He looked at me, though, with a puzzled glance. Suddenly, a duck scrambled through from the other room. An oppressive silence followed once the animal darted off. The sounds of sheep grazing far away reached us on their tiny feet, but that was all.

"Stay here," my father said. He pointed to a bench. "Wait."

He looked into the other room, then went out and around the hut. I saw him listening. Finally, he returned and sat beside me.

"We will have to wait," he said.

It is impossible now to remember how long we sat before hearing the approach of my people. It was late afternoon.

My father rose quickly and greeted them from the door. I stood behind him, peering from beneath his raised arm. A young man and woman walked gingerly up the slope, an old and bleached man between them. My grandfather was unable to walk without their support. He looked like a long white shell, seaweed clinging unmercifully to the thin furrows of calcium. His head hung against a white cotton shirt, streaked brown and yellow; the crotch of his pants seemed permanently stained with red and yellow.

When I saw him like that, I gasped. I thought, at first, that he had been hit by a car. They carried him in like so much rope.

My father held the cloth against his mouth as he looked closely at his father. The couple sat the old man down in a chair, then stood back.

"He's very sick," the man said.

My father leaned close as he spoke. "How long has he been like this?"

"Two years," the woman answered.

"Can he understand?"

"He hasn't been able to for five months now. Two years ago, he had a stroke and stopped walking. Last year another stroke sealed his mouth. Then, about five months ago, the light from his eyes disappeared in the night."

The man sat beside my grandfather. "He will die soon."

"Who takes care of him?"

"María and me."

"Do you need money, Juan?"

The man didn't answer and I felt deeply ashamed for my father's impoliteness. How could he ask at a time like that?

The woman sighed and rubbed her hands together. "Well, the children don't have much to eat. They work in the fields until dark. It's a very hard life."

"I'll give you money before I go."

"Oh, thank you, Don Miguel." The woman clasped my father's hand.

"Thank you," the man said. "Poor Ezíquiel will die soon. It takes too much time to care for him. It's better if he dies quickly. We take him to the field with us, but it takes time."

"He loved his field," my father said.

"At first his eyes held the old silver when we sat him in his field. We made a seat by the coconuts. He liked them best."

The woman continued for her husband. "But now, Don Miguel, his eyes are empty and still. We don't take him there anymore."

"Why not?" I blurted out angrily.

They smiled at me. Smiled down at me.

"My son..."

"Oh, yes," the man said. He smiled again and put his hand out. "Marco. I'm your grandfather's grandson. By another woman," he quickly added. "This is María, my wife."

I shook his hand. The woman hugged me from behind, her lips pressing into my hair.

"He looks like you," she said to my father.

"Some say like his mother." The cloth across his face twitched with each word.

I couldn't stand listening to them. I wanted them to shut up, to realize that they were talking about Ezíquiel, my grandfather, my history and my blood, not some goddamned stranger!

My voice pushed weakly past my clenched throat, where I grabbed it before it broke wetly. I sat near Ezíquiel, ignoring the others, and looked into his face. This face I had never seen before. His mouth opened and spittle ran into his shirt. The liquid turned brown as it spread. I wanted to cry. The old man farted loudly against his chair.

"It's too hard to care for him," María said in response.

My father pushed the cones more firmly into his nose.

Juan stood and lifted a water gourd to his lips. "He'll die soon," he said before drinking.

"No!" I shouted.

They stared at me.

"No!" I grabbed his shoulders. "Oh, Grandfather, I love you." I cried then, unafraid of what the others would think. "Grandfather, please." My tears smelled of blood against my cheeks. "Please, *Abuelo*, listen to me. Speak to me, please. Let me understand!"

His gaze lifted up to my strong emotion, a sudden light coming from deep within those black pupils. I knew he understood me, then. He felt me. He recognized me from across the years, across the miles and miles of fervent and disconsolate blood. Emotion was the bridge of years. Oh, I knew it *then*.

"Yes!" I said, the sound barely escaping my throat.

He rose stiffly, majestically. I trembled visibly, tears choking my breath as his mouth opened before me with the slowness of dawn.

I waited for his words like a fledgling, watched him magically stand. The others, too, seemed amazed at this phoenix strength. I heard María suck her breath in quickly.

Ezíquiel's hand raised and he pointed at me.

"Oh, yes," I whispered again. "Yes, yes!"

"Raul," he said sonorously. "Raul!"

His eyes sparkled like the village oil lamps, sparkled like the wings of parrots rising from the fields. And he sobbed.

Tears rolled from those dark eyes and fell to the ground with the clatter and clicking of obsidian teeth. The long sweeping smell of the salt and sea filled the room and I saw that his tears were exact miniatures of the shells that followed me through the streets of Indiana, Michigan, the United States.

"Who's Raul?" I asked, breathlessly, my own tears the cauldron of my face.

No one answered. They moved, instead, toward the wrinkled old man who swayed dangerously. They brought his arms down like broken sticks, and guided him back to the chair, back to his mannequin pose and wooden stare.

"Ignore him," Juan said. "When he's tired, he babbles. Just ignore him."

That was that: Ignore the shell and bone.

UNDER AN ICE MOON

▼

I WAS BESIDE MYSELF WHEN I GOT THE GRANT.
Others had applied, surely with strong proposals. It was a chance for
something different. I suppose the Guatemala Maya fired the judge's interests:
strange calendars and glyphs. For me, a low growl of hummingbird wings
beating rapidly through the imagination. That was what I had read in a
magazine, and that was what had sent me to the library for days, to the
typewriter for hours.

"How the hell?" was what Jenny said. "A novelist?" She felt the sting of
injustice. It was her field.

"The times are changing, I suppose."

"To simplicity!"

"Institutions are getting interdisciplinary."

She sulked all week. I didn't have the heart to show her the *National
Geographic* that talked of the Kekchí Maya like they were hobbits. I could not
confess that I peeked through her notes for summary statements and bibliog-
raphy. I brought her little things instead. A collection of stories by Albizúrez
Palma. But it was one she'd been looking for for seven months. Wednesday,
I called spontaneously, rashly, out of the clear, to say I love you, but the
answering machine kept her free to work undisturbed. Chocolates on Thursday, when she decided to diet. On Saturday I said, Honey, let's quit working and
go eat at that Darbar Restaurant you like so much. She said she had nothing
to wear. The laundry was overdue.

"Anything," I said. "Let me do something nice for you."

"Something nice?" she said. "Something nice? Something nice for *me?*" She went into the bedroom and closed the door. I thought she might be crying, so I waited for the first hard edge to break free of her before going in. She came out wearing some little bit we'd gotten at *Private Fashions.*

"We'll eat in," she said.

She made love to me until I couldn't keep my eyes open. She made love to me until I had no joy even in her beautiful hair matted across her breasts. Then she sat on me. I pleaded with her, but she yanked me up by the shoulders. She shook me like a child to keep me awake.

I whimpered.

She kissed my neck, scratched my nipples.

"Please," I said. "Honey, I give up. I give up. Please."

"Do you need my help?" she asked.

"Yes. Lord."

"Do I get a by-line?"

"Yes."

"Is it fair, John Beattie?"

"No, my raisin. My love." My God. All I wanted was sleep.

"Hah!" she said.

She got up to shower, leaving me to mumble pathetically that it wasn't my fault.

We were squared by the time we left. We decided to go first to Mérida, Yucatán, where she knew a few people, travel down to Chetumal and into Belize. She had made this trip recently, at her own expense, before we'd met, and enjoyed pointing out things anthropologists thrive on: the change of living from Mérida to Chetumal, shifts in dress, the increase of blacks in traditionally non-black areas. Once across the border, she pointed out the changes in music, and her new interest: the Mayas who spoke not only their native tongue and Spanish, but a Caribbean English as well.

I knew she was just keeping the truth of my grant alive.

On the bus from Belize City to Benque Viejo, we passed three Americans lurching through the scrub by the road. Boffing through the brush like they never knew the sixties had ended. I heard Jen sigh.

"You know," she said angrily, "there are books that say the Mayas are one of the lost tribes of Israel? There are books that say that they came from Atlantis. There are people who think Quetzalcoatl was Jesus Christ. If the Mayas aren't cute, they're mystical. God, I hate that. People come looking for some kind of Carlos Castanedan magic. Do you know that I read a book about the Mayas written by a woman who had spent exactly two weeks in a Yucatán hotel? I've studied a tiny area for years. I'll never understand it all. No one can. Ever! Where do these superficial writers get off? Leeches!" Then she looked at me as if she had caught the barest taste of something old and unpleasant in her mouth.

"You're saving me from that," I said.

"A grant to study Maya culture! For crying out loud. I put in a request, you know. I spent quite a bit of time on that *app*. I have plenty of publications. I have years. Isn't it just more than a little unfair?"

"Are you getting hungry?"

"Don't worry, though. You'll be famous. You'll add to that great storehouse of misinformation. You'll have your poems and stories!"

I knew enough not to speak. This was something coming from deeper than I wanted to delve.

The bus stopped in San Ignacio, where we took a taxi to the *frontera*. From there, we walked down from the office with our backpacks and across the river to Melchor de Mencos for the bus to Flores Petén.

Jenny did most of the talking. My Spanish was weak.

The trip took hours on the ragged, dusty road. We passed military outposts with names like *Infierno* and *Xibalbá*, where the infamous Kaibil regiments toughed it out. I jotted down all names in my notebook. These were the forces quashing rebellions. They were the government arms, muscular and zealous. Gorillas. Bloodletters. Jen read my notes without comment, or commented without words: a hissing on her tongue, eyes rolling up.

In Flores, we checked into the Hotel Maya and quickly changed to swim the lake that washed up to the very back door. The island of Flores was sinking. Perhaps beneath the weight of tourism. It felt delicious to rid ourselves of the dust that seemed to have filled us to the very nooks of our bones. Jenny swam out further than I dared to, then dove under. The initial ripples from her dive smoothed to form a platter of sunset. When she shot up, suddenly and much closer, her hair was like a crystalline shawl and her face, shoulders and small breasts, seemed to yearn for sky. A cormorant lanced into the water just behind her, so that it appeared for an instant to be actually descending through her upturned mouth and into her body.

"The quiet is fabulous," she said with such peacefulness that I wished for a thousand birds descending through her lips.

We took a van the next day to Tikal. At first, Jen told me what she knew as we climbed each temple. She related history and cultural tidbits so well that other tourists walked close by, but as we continued through the vast ruins, she said less and less. At Temple Five, a swarm of bees sent us flailing down the roughly cleared pyramid.

We saved Temple Three for last to enjoy the unexcavated face and to rest at the top, away from the usual visitor. High above the jungle canopy, we each wore helmets of silence and rocked privately to the swells of that great sea greening beneath us.

I finally spoke. "Maybe the death squads are the new sacrificers," I said. My own phrases in the taxi about the Kaibil had come back to me. Somewhere in my mind there were these glyphs of a woman pulling a rope through her tongue, an elite above her.

"Sh," Jen said. Her eyes were closed, her palms softly together on her lap. "Please, let's just sit here. Let's not try to understand anything."

That night, Jen pulled me to her. We made love on the edge of pain, her eyes full of a strange and private constellation.

We stayed in Petén only a few days before going on by bus to Lake Atitlán, far to the southwest. My proposal said I would investigate correlations between present Tzutujil folklore and the *Popol Vuh*, a "Maya bible." I had no experience in any of this, but a fiction writer should be able to create experience, from nothing if need be. And here was something, not nothing.

"Let's skip Panajachel," she said in the capital, where our busline ended. "I can't handle the tourists. It's all more of the same."

She laughed, then, at some secret joke. When I pressed her, she said that in Panajachel you could spend eighty quetzales for a room and not even get a hammock. Then she laughed again, triggering into some past event.

"Don't they have beds?" I asked.

"Geez," she said and turned to one of the boys unloading our bags. She got the line to Atitlán from him. We walked fifteen blocks to 14th Avenue and 6th

Street and waited. I fell asleep leaning against my bag, my feet sprawling across the sidewalk.

By the time I awoke, Jenny had taken care of everything for us. "Cerro de Oro," she said. "We'll take this to San Lucas Tolimán then catch the bus to Santiago Atitlán. Cerro de Oro is midway between San Lucas and Santiago. We'll get off and walk half an hour."

"Sounds out of the way."

"A tourist there is fair game," she said, balling up her fist.

"Show me," I said.

"It's not on our map. Thank God!"

We arrived just before dawn, the mountains dense with fog, the air too cold for what I had worn. I tried to hold Jen to me, but she walked faster. A woman with two children was making the same trip. She quickly tied some packets into the ornate scarf slung across her shoulder and hussled her ducklings ahead of us.

Jen didn't even try to get any help from her.

"Why is she scared of us?" I said.

"Well, who the hell are we?"

"Friends!" I said. "Isn't it obvious? Tell her we're here to do research. And slow down."

"Oh, lady," she said in English, "excuse me. We want to inspect your life. Can we look at your daughter's teeth, please? Who are your Gods? Have any folktales you can tell us? It'll only take a minute."

"I see."

The road—path—led us down from the main road and around a large hill called Cerro de Oro. It was just light enough to see here and there a man working his field with a hoe. One man lit a cigarette and quietly watched us until we passed from sight.

"So what do we do?"

"Once in the village, we ask for Tomás Xiquín. According to the bus driver, he's supposed to have rooms we can rent."

"And if he doesn't?"

"Then we see if anyone else has a room. If worse comes to worst, we go to Santiago and get a hotel."

"How far's that?"

"An hour. Hour-and-a-half."

"Walking?" I said. I was already short of breath.

Jenny wiggled her eyebrows.

We came upon a small rise just above the village. Paths criss-crossed between huts and compounds of huts. Once in Cerro de Oro, gatherings of children giggled at everything we did. Adults seemed disinterested. One woman had a dark breast out from a fold in her *huipil*. Her baby slept in the cloth sling around her shoulder, one tiny hand pressed against the breast the way a cat will sleep with paws tensed out.

Jen approached her for information, while I jotted down my first impressions. She looked back sharply, as if I were invading people's privacy or fulfilling some pet peeve of hers.

We continued toward Santiago, according to directions. It seemed we would leave the village altogether when we finally came across another clutch of huts by the lake. Jen called out for Tomás Xiquín.

A toothless woman came from the hut, followed by very young children who scattered around the cornstalk fence to peer at us. She greeted us by saying something like *Utz Awach* and pointing her index finger to heaven.

We greeted her in Spanish.

The woman preferred Jen's Spanish over mine, so she told the woman that we were tourists. We wanted a quiet place to stay. The lake is beautiful. We had heard that the people of Cerro de Oro were warm and friendly. That a señor Xiquín might have a room for rent. She bargained with the woman. We settled into a cinderblock room with a single hammock tied up through bolts in the walls. There was one chest of drawers, a laminated wood dresser with one end propped up by a rock. The floor was dirt, the slat door almost closed.

"Home," she said, then chuckled at me.

"Don't you worry about me," I said. "Big deal, so we go outside to piss and there're no chairs."

She swung into the hammock. "You ever sleep in one of these?"

"I've napped in a few."

She smiled. "We'll be close," she said, her eyebrows wiggling again.

I tried to picture us. She did a nifty flip out of the hammock and unpacked. I took the bottom drawer.

Once the sun had risen a quarter into the sky, we warmed up enough to walk along the lake with our sleeves rolled. We walked toward the village so people could get used to seeing us, and bought some bread and *Gallo* beer to take back. Everyone seemed friendly enough, though not overly talkative. Other than the short walk, we stayed to ourselves. Jen warned against rushing things. For me, the walk gave me plenty of notes on the way houses were made, the kinds of animals allowed to roam free, and a long list of plants I would have to look up later.

Jen shook her head. "When you write out your story, you'll just name the plants as if you always knew what they were. Isn't that the way with everything? The great faking of knowledge. Dazzle them with surfaces!"

"It's for realism. It draws the reader in, makes him think you know what you're talking about."

She nodded in that slow and slack-jawed way to emphasize her disbelief or disgust, I'm not sure which.

Xiquín finally came by near nightfall. When I pulled open the door, some of the children drew closer to him. The old woman squatted off to the side.

"*Utz Awach*," he said. He wore the traditional short pants and extremely colorful sash to keep the pants up.

I offered him one of our beers, but he refused. Jen insisted until he took it. It made me feel like she really did know about all this. I knew then that I would never tell her the truth of my grant.

All of us squatted or sat by the door. Jen gave me a nod as Tomás pushed the long tassels of the belt down between his legs to sit. In the same motion, he fanned the cloth behind him so that his pants did not touch the ground. We talked, awkwardly, for an hour: about the beauty of the lake, about distances to the various villages. We asked where to buy food. He told us we could get fresh fish from the men who sleep in their dugout boats, live chickens from anyone. If we wanted meat we would have to go to either Santiago or San Lucas. There, we could also get other things we needed. His wife, the old woman, would make our tortillas if we wanted. Our conversation had turned to my questions about the village when Tomás calmly asked me how we were going to cook. I shrugged, a little embarrassed. I suddenly realized that he had said *live* chickens. He explained that the rent included board.

Finally, Jenny said she wanted to sleep. We excused ourselves and *almost* closed the door. Jenny told me to look in the *Popol Vuh* for the episode of the

Hero Twins turning their half-brothers into monkeys. "Look for the pants' tassels turning into tails," she said.

"What's it mean?"

"You should read the book," she said flatly.

Later, as I rocked uncomfortably in the hammock with Jen asleep in my arms, I noticed the occasional glint of children's eyes like muted fireflies in the crack of the door.

That next day, I went out early, tape recorder and notebook in hand, determined to sit in the middle of the village so that nervousness over us would end, and to get some preliminary notes. I left Jen bathing in the turquoise water of the lake and warning me to go slow.

I started with a storeowner. He smoked heavily and seemed not to want to go much past saying numbers in Tzutujil. I wrote them down. A missing tooth made certain words indecipherable, so I bought us some beers. I took one of his cigarettes. We progressed to his naming cigarette and beer in Tzutujil. He even named matches. We smiled a lot at each other. It was a start.

In one of the cavernous spaces between words, both of us looking awkwardly for something to say, I saw a series of half pint bottles labeled *Venado*. When he caught the direction of my gaze, I asked him what they were. He cracked the seal and pushed one across the wood counter. Rather than try to explain that I didn't want it, I pointed as if to offer him the bottle. He reached back and cracked open another, this time thanking me. From beneath the counter, he drew out a plastic dish full of crude salt and a lime which he quickly quartered. It was rum, drunk, apparently, in half bottle swigs followed by salt and lime. The liquor was a whole fish swallowed backwards, the clear scales rasping slowly down the esophagus. In the gut, it was a sea urchin of heat. After the fourth drink, somehow that tiny fish went down head first and the urchin had unfurled its spines into each tributary of the body. My notes were abandoned. Our Spanish was abandoned. He spoke Tzutujil and I spoke English.

When I left, staggering my way back to Jen, I saw an ancient woman staring disapprovingly at me. She grasped the arm of a child the way, I'm sure, she would have wanted to pull me aside. Later, under Jenny's scowl, I felt even greater affinity with that young boy. I tried to contain the school of fish in my head.

"I made connections," I said emphatically. "I connected with the villagers."
She would say nothing. In the hammock, she turned away, her teeth tight.
By the end of the second week, my notebook had several pages of notes from
Tomás Xiquín. He told me about various crops and the seasons for each. He
told me about the reaping of black corn, the sowing of beans, the problems
with growing coffee. From Chepe Poc, the storeowner, I learned about trucks
that delivered groceries. He told me of a Catholic priest murdered years earlier
in Santiago for his participation with the community. He said there were
guerrillas fighting from bases in Volcan Tolimán, the cloud-wreathed volcano
blocking the horizon for Cerro de Oro.

My pages slowly filled with secret wars fought on the paths leading in and
out of the main villages. Machetes glinted in the night, the leap of gunflash
illuminated my notebook. Jenny slowly learned this particular Mayan language. In one week, she could give appropriate hellos, thanks, goodbyes and
polite requests. She recorded the casual tales of women as they wove *huipils*
and skirts. She quietly practiced her Tzutujil vocabulary within the folds of the
hammock while I invented the union of farmers and their arming. I preferred
the hardness of the wall against my back when I wrote. She preferred the
privacy of the fine mesh. We worked like this in the evenings: apart in mind,
yet together in the same tiny room.

"These people are poor," I said. "They need a revolution! Half of them don't
even have running water. They bust ass for subsistence. How could they be
happy?"

She peered at me. Her whole face seemed soft in the dull light of the oil lamp.
Her eyes were darkened and I expected her to respond. Instead, she shifted
her position, and her eyes suddenly shone brilliant red like a cat's eyes netting
light.

"A woman invited us to her daughter's first birthday party," she said. Then
she turned from me. Her hair fell from behind her shoulders and concealed
her eyes. The lamp brought out the slight touches of red in her hair.

"When?" I asked.

She spoke from the private alcove of her hair. "Sunday afternoon."

"Should we go?"

"Yes. It's in Santiago."

"What's the matter?"

She shook her head briefly, so the remaining strands fell from around her shoulder to further cup her face.

I got up from the floor and put my arm around her. "What's the matter?" "The woman's had three children die of disease," she said.

"That's too bad."

Jen nodded.

"Should we take a gift?"

But Jenny continued: "She asked me if I had children and when I said no, she was startled. She stared at me for a long, long time, John. She was measuring my age. I told her I would never have children. I told her that my life had made a turn for a profession. I told her that I was an anthropologist; I studied human culture. I told her my profession was husband, child and life. I told her I would never have a child and then she hugged her daughter so hard that I thought she would swallow her up. After the longest time without a word between us, she asked me to join her daughter's birthday party."

"They have hard lives," I said.

She closed her eyes as if I hadn't understood, then fell protectively into the hammock, back into her privacy.

I slid alongside her. Her hand cupped my ear; she buried her face in my neck.

"I want us to discover sex again," she said. "I want us to make love like the first time. Not the first time hot, but the first time love. Frightened. All the world full of unfairness and us honest and quiet because of it."

I kissed her, stroked her. With eyes closed, she brought her warm and open mouth to mine. We made love slowly. There seemed nothing in the heavens but our patient undressing of each other and the gentle enfolding of our limbs. When I entered her, she collapsed into me, quietly, trying to touch every part of her body against mine. Our motions were close, secretive, so that enveloped in one another, we undulated the hammock like a single body.

Even before I came, she coughed softly against my shoulder. Her teeth grabbed my skin. I came with the barest sound, too, and tried to kiss her mouth. But she turned to keep me from seeing her tears.

"Did I hurt you?" I said.

She shook her head.

"I don't understand," I said. I then remembered a woman long ago who had cried after orgasm. She was a dancer. She had gotten angry at my concern.

"It's nothing," Jen whispered. "Hold me."

"What's wrong?"

"Nothing. It's okay."

"I don't understand."

She smiled at me, burbled a short laugh, then pulled my face against her. In the hollow of my neck she said, "That's okay. The trick, I guess, is to never question." Her words came like a cotton dabbing of my skin.

Sunday, we walked to the main road for the bus to Santiago. A half dozen others waited with us. The upper slopes of the volcanoes were clouded. A flock of parrots screeched far above. All of us sat quietly by the road, some poking their toes into the dirt, some chewing grass, some snapping twigs into tiny pieces. No one spoke in that peace. Jenny's leg touched mine. She had her head back, her face to the sky, full of a happiness I hadn't seen in her since I got my grant.

"What are you thinking?" I asked. It had to be good.

Without moving, she said, "Absolutely nothing."

The bus was crammed with people, and dustier inside than out. We stood in the aisle by the driver, barely able to move. Only occasionally did I catch a glimpse of the turquoise water of Lake Atitlán, and that only when the bus swung down like a great nodding head because of potholes.

When a strange chatter spread among us, I squirmed down to see the bus from Santiago stopped ahead. Its passengers surrounded a man lying in the road. Clearly, there had been a death, but when we came closer and saw the large circle of flesh ripped away from the man's chest, everyone knew it was a vicious killing. His tattered shirt whipped across the wound.

The other bus driver explained that they had found the body half an hour earlier. He pointed below the road and described how the corpse had been dragged up the hill and onto the road to be discovered. Most of them knew the man. It was his field of corn by the road. He had worked for the police in Santiago.

Our driver said he would notify officials in Santiago and hurried us back onto the bus. All conversation ended. I tried asking the driver about the corpse, but I was so anxious and disturbed that my Spanish was even more miserable and confusing than usual. Jenny would not ask anything for me.

"It's got to be a political death. Find out!"

"It's none of our business," she said angrily. "We don't need to know. All we'll know is opinions—at best!"

I tried again. I fumbled a question about the guerrillas.

"I don't know," the driver answered.

"Help me!"

But Jen turned her head.

"Are you scared?"

"Think what you want," she said with finality.

The news of the murder had reached Santiago. A few people stood on a street discussing it, some only paused for a brief comment. We passed a woman sobbing so loudly that she must have been related to the deceased. All the time, Jenny walked doggedly to her friend's home. She would not tolerate my stopping to question.

"Damnit," I said. "What's the matter with asking?"

She walked so fast that I nearly ran to keep pace.

"Nothing," she said. "I just don't want bits. We can't know what happened. Damnit, I'm afraid we'll think we know. You'll pass this on and people'll think you know the truth. No one ever gets it. I guess it's nothing or everything, and everything is impossible."

"And what the hell does that mean?"

"Please, John. I'm not stopping. You do what you want. You can keep the charade up, but I'm not."

At the small block house, the guests were already seated around tables pushed together. We were introduced as tourists, Jenny as a friend of the mother, María Choy. I quickly discovered that they had all heard of the murder, some had known the man well.

I said I was horrified.

They consoled me. The Fire Chief, a round man with gold-capped teeth, shook his head knowingly. A woman doctor, seated with her husband, said that it must have been shocking to see death so close. She said that they had gotten used to it.

María Choy bounced the girl on her knee and asked her husband to begin serving the guests. Jenny asked if she could help. María's husband, José, smiled no.

I said, "It's an unfortunate life when people get used to murder." Jenny kicked her heel into my ankle.

The doctor's husband laughed stiffly.

"Every fifteen days there's a new body," another man said.

"Is it political?" I asked. Jenny held her hands flat on the table and stared at me. "Is it political," I repeated, louder.

Several of the guests answered in unison: "No one knows."

"He was a commissioner," the doctor said finally.

"Guerrillas, then?"

José Choy spoke as he placed spoons before all of us. "Or maybe the army just wants the people to believe so."

"Who knows," several repeated again.

Jenny had grown silent. Her hands lay stiff and awkward on the edge of the table. Her gaze hardened somewhere in front of her.

José Choy brought out small bowls of a chile and chicken soup. María proudly said that it was a traditional meal. Her sisters brought out beers and Coca-Cola. The baby lolled sleepily on her mother's shoulder.

"Doesn't anyone try to find out what happens?" I said.

They smiled politely. They ate the soup slowly. It was all we would eat.

I persisted: "Where are the guerrillas?"

"Up the volcanoes," the Fire Chief said.

A grisly old man spoke out from the end of the table. "Or the military wants us to think that. It is the army that kills people after curfew. It is always the same for us." The man settled back, his forearms crossed, his body hunched forward.

"Foolishness," the Fire Chief said. "I am the one to get these bodies. There's too much made of politics. Last month, I went to collect the body of a woman in Pasanahí. Her husband had chopped off her arms with his machete because of infidelity. He threw himself from the *cerros*, but his wife was not dead. She is still living. No, there's too much made of politics. Jealousy. Drunkenness. Greed. These are the armies and guerrillas fighting in our villages."

"But how can you say that?" I said. "There have been documented cases of the army killing people."

All of them stared. Jenny hung her head.

"There are guerrillas! They're fighting for human rights. For *your* lives.

They should be supported, not thought of as stories. At least you should find out the truth."

Jenny looked up at the faces around us, at the small girl in her mother's lap. In English, she growled, "Stop it!"

"I'm sorry," I said to everyone, "but if there are deaths, something should be done. People should unite and find out what's going on."

They said nothing. They fiddled with their soups. María Choy placed the girl in her husband's arms and left the room.

"*Lo siento*," Jenny said aloud.

The conversation ended: only the dull rasping of spoon against ceramic. María returned to sit again at the head of the table. José carefully passed her the sleepy girl. María stroked her daughter's hair, stroked the chubby cheeks with the back of her fingers. She kissed the girl's hair with her eyes closed.

Outside, Jenny yanked my arm. "Who the hell do you think you are?"

"What do you mean?" I said.

"You don't know? You seriously don't know?" Her face was a snarl of lines, confused and bitter.

"No!"

"Damn you," she said, and marched toward the bus.

She did not speak to me on the way back. I gave up trying and stared at the dying sunlight out over the volcanoes opposite the lake. Already there was mist in the highest reaches.

I tried again on the walk to the room, but she pulled further ahead whenever I stepped beside her. We walked for forty minutes that way: Jenny ten to fifteen feet in front, both of us walking at a fast clip, the moon ascending icily. A few people living along the path watched us, their expressions full of questions.

Finally, in the room, I would not let her take her bag without talking to me. I held the strap. A brief tug-of-war followed, then she backed up.

"Are you keeping me from what is mine?" she said.

"Look, all I want is to know what's going on. Can't you talk to me?"

"Okay," she said. "Okay. You have a responsibility. You have no right to come into a place and think you know more than these people. You have no right to say they can't be happy, or to invent a whole solution to problems you can't ever understand. You cannot go around being facile and simplistic and blasting things out when people may think you're some kind of authority. And

it was a birthday party, for crying out loud. Don't you see?"
She looked up at me. "You just don't get it, do you?"

"And you do?" I said. "Maybe I did wrong because it was a birthday party, but what I said is right. It is right!—You're just jealous because you didn't get the grant. You've been bitching since the day I got it. Did it ever occur to you that I just might deserve it? You're not the only one who can write about these people. You've been jealous because I happened to deserve it and you didn't!"

And she slapped me hard enough for the tears to start up in one eye. She stood back, fist up in my face, a hurricane of words inside her. Her mouth moved grotesquely, then she turned away without a sound. She snatched the backpack from the floor.

She walked the path toward Cerro de Oro. She walked twenty yards, almost hidden by night, before I took a step forward.

"Honey, please," I shouted.

She brushed her hand behind her, whisking me away, whisking who knows what away, and walked on. I thought she'd cool down, see that I wasn't all wrong. Come back to me. All she needed was to cool off.

I watched her disappear up the dark road. I stood under that moon, waiting. Four bats jagged across the light. Somewhere an owl called. But the next time I heard Jenny's voice was back home in Clowerston. I telephoned her office. She had already moved her things from my apartment.

"The key's in the mail," she said. "Don't call again. I expect you not to make a scene on campus."

"What about us?" I said. "I looked a long time for you down there. You created a big hassle for me, you know. I searched for quite a bit and, with my Spanish, it wasn't easy. Don't you owe me something? Don't you owe *us* something?"

"I'm seeing someone else."

"So soon? You're lying. I don't believe it."

"Two men. A dozen. Anyone, but you. I've changed too."

"Too?"

"Too?" she said incredulously. "I guess you're right! You've always been blind to the needs of others."

"I don't understand," I said. "Please. How could this happen? When did it? How could it happen overnight?"

"Goodbye," she answered. "Write out your little trip like you're a hero. Act like you know even one thing about those people. Write like you know anyfuckingthing!"

And she hung up.

Not another word.

No apology.

Nothing.

CROSSING THE BORDER

▼

WHEN RAÚL CÁSCARA DIED NO ONE BELIEVED it. Raúl was the caretaker for a chestnut grove outside the village of Motagua, but he was endowed with the ability to fake almost anything. Each year at Festival, he pretended to be some new and wondrous thing. The previous year, Raúl had climbed a tree and spread a scintillating pair of wings behind him. The children squealed as he leaped from a branch and flew erratically some twenty feet. It was the largest butterfly the village had seen. Only three years earlier, Raúl flabbergasted the village by becoming the living night sky. He had enticed fireflies to cover his body from head to toes, then he stood atop a house like the very heavens, twinkling ebulliently in opaline hues. Rumor had it that he would venture to become a nautilus at the coming festival.

So, when old Doña María happened upon Raúl as he lay slumped over a rock by the salt river, she first thought he was practicing for the festival. "You make all our children happy," Doña María said. When he made no answer, she smiled wisely and left him in peace. She came into the village and mentioned what she had seen. A few older boys went out to watch, curious as to how Raúl practiced his art of fakery, and pleased that the rumors they had helped spread were proven right. Finding him just as Doña María had said, they sat along the upper bank and watched Raúl in his craft.

Raúl was a small man, even by the standards of the village. He had black curly hair, cut roughly above his collar, and a tangled beard that grew in patches across his chin. His mustache curled upward from his lip and thinned to a thistle just an inch from either eye. Both his spindly legs dipped like roots into the brackish river. One sandal was off. In one hand he held a thread of vine that curved and sewed through the rocks of the bank, slithered up the embankment, and ascended a grisly fig tree. He held nothing in his other hand.

Several hours later, the boys grew tired and left with a shout of encouragement. It was a sign of Raúl's great concentration and prowess that he did not answer the good-byes of his young admirers.

Doña María, returning by the Cunumán river on the way to her home in the hills, called out to Raúl. "You are a joy to us all, Raúl Cáscara. No!" she added quickly, "do not get up."

It wasn't until the fourth day that the village suddenly fluttered with the realization of Raúl's condition. A murmur of understanding whispered through each person like the chill of an autumnal wind. "He's not practicing to be a nautilus," they all said. "He's practicing to be a dead man!"

"Bravo!" Doña María shouted, along with others.

All of them—free of any envy for Raúl's great skill—agreed that his genius lay not only in his versatility and unpredictability, but in his persuasiveness, as well.

Séptimo Tzuí, the coroner, leaned in close and checked Raúl carefully. "This is the most convincing portrayal of death imaginable," he finally proclaimed.

The cheers deafened the woods, so that the birds lay hushed on the sleeves of trees.

"We must honor this man," Séptimo said.

"We must give him the title," others said.

So, fourteen days before the Festival of the Saints of Our Shame and Delight, the village named Raúl as the Lord of Festival and Chief Customs Officer of the Spirit of Good Life. As such, he presided over the committee for the arrangements of Festival, and was obliged to dine with this family and that family until there was virtually no time left for his own needs.

While this did not go unappreciated by the others, it was generally assumed that the title was such an honor as to trivialize the inconvenience. Any sensible man would accept the difficulties for the prestige. They were pleased that Raúl did not complain. Moreover, some considered elevating Raúl to the status of Greatest Chief Customs Officer of the Spirit of Good Life because he performed his duties without the slightest complaint or bragging or comment whatsoever. Others, those of less generous spirits, complained that it would be unfair to give Raúl that honor as he was practicing death and was, therefore, unable to utter a sound. They argued, as some are prone to do, the extenuating circumstances and not the deed itself. But this opened the way for what was later to occur.

As had been done since the coronation, the eldest sons of the hosting family carried Raúl's body to the house and set him at the head of the table. Then, after all the toasts in honor of the Lord of Festival, the family ate in reverential silence. In this case, however, Raúl presided over the family of his friend, Diego Tzunún. A family, it was said, that had claims to being the very first settlers of Motagua, laying further claim to being the direct descendants of the great Guatemalan prince, Kicab. Later, it was said that these very honors gave Diego and his family the necessary vision to see the truth. Diego said that it was due to his long association with Raúl. The truth will never be known—can never be known—but that evening as the family ate and noted how their esteemed guest solidified his genius by refusing to eat, Diego leaned forward and observed aloud how Raúl seemed changed. Disturbed and curious, the others leaned close.

It was true. Raúl did seem different. "He is not happy," Diego observed. And soon, the others in the village saw it clearly enough, as well.

That very evening Séptimo, Chirón and María Teresa tried to coax the problem from Raúl himself. They spoke to him while many others waited out in the main avenue for news of their Lord. Children shifted restlessly in the arms of anxious parents. Goats and donkeys lounged less comfortably in the street. Even so, there was nothing said, and no way to pry open the ingenious mouth of Raúl Cáscara.

It was as if the people needed only that one night to break some invisible barrier. Every day afterward, someone noticed another difference in Raúl. Some days, like the crescendoing of birdsong in the jungle, differences beyond count were noted. Perhaps Diego's first observation sparked an over-zealousness in the village. Individuals would look closely at Raúl, hoping to enter the ranks of the astute by finding some change. Young men would call out with the slightest provocation and claim that now Raúl had the hairs of his mustache curling upward, or that he was now a small man with a scraggly beard. The older men and women would correct them and point out that it was their age that made them notice the obvious, things unknown only to the self-centered wonder of youth. Still, real differences were seen. Now Raúl had a faraway look in his eyes, as if trying to make out something just visible on the horizon; now his fingers were straight as if in humble adulation; now his mouth held the righteous smile of *Venceremos*—that straight line of wisdom.

All total, twenty real differences were noted by the eve of the Festival of the Saints of Our Shame and Delight. And on the day of the festival, those differences seemed to stand like quills as Raúl rode on the Chair of Light and Retribution. Carried through the village, his presence blessed the will and virtue of all who embraced the Good Life of the Blessed Rattan, Broken Canes, Rotten Canes, Gumarcaah: nexus of Guatemala. And because the look of change hung about Raúl, even people who had never known him, or those who knew him through description alone, could see that something was not as it should be.

Then materialized the idea of offering a reward to discover what troubled Raúl. The festival, as always, attracted men and women of immense and varied talents. There were merchants and entertainers, diviners and shamans, magicians and priests, evangelists and devils, pardoners and possessed, laymen and mother-fathers. There were the many families that traveled from festival to festival, showing off the latest gadgetry from the capital. But even as Diego and others discussed the reward, a very old man approached and said that he would find the truth from Raúl.

"You have noticed our Lord of Festival?" Séptimo asked with some surprise.

"Yes," the man said, paring a fingernail with a knife. "How could one not notice?"

"What we mean," Diego said, "is do you see anything out of the ordinary with him?"

"Yes, I have said. How can one not notice him? But I can discover what problem he has."

"How, old man?" Diego asked.

"My name, *joven*, is Juan Aguacero!"

"How can you help us, then?"

"There are many things that I can do," he said. "I have found the way to cure certain cancerous wounds and to stop the flight of birds. I can even sing to the monkeys of Petén and make them play their flutes."

"Fine, Juan Aguacero," Séptimo said, "but we are concerned here with our friend and Lord of Festival."

"You people are very slow in understanding, aren't you? Haven't I just told you that I can do all manner of things? Didn't you just hear that I will help?"

Séptimo and Diego looked at one another in surprise.

"All I want," the man continued, "is for you to arrange things as I ask."

María Teresa and Chirón agreed to try. "What can it hurt?" Chirón said.

"When the sun sets," Juan Aguacero began, "have a place ready in this manner: Gather close friends and have them sweep a circle clean. Bring a pot of boiling gum and cacao to this place. Bring a bag of fresh clippings from the toenails of a young boy and girl. Paint the girl's nails red. There must be twenty full clippings!"

Juan Aguacero stopped and put a hand to his mouth.

"Is that all?" María Teresa asked after some time.

"If I had meant to say more, I would have."

María Teresa looked down into the eyes of the *sanjorín*. "You are a very disagreeable old man."

He cocked his head. "I am doing this without reward."

"Why?" blurted Diego.

The old man smiled wisely. "To expect everything answered is foolish. To want everything answered is childish."

Chirón stepped quickly between Diego and Juan Aguacero. "Don't worry, it will all be taken care of. We will have everything ready."

"Of course," Juan Aguacero said, and turned to the festival.

With hours left before sunset, there was still plenty of time for both the preparations and the festivities of the day. So that close to the hour, the friends of Raúl—and there were many—gathered at the square to brush away a clear circle. They built a wood fire in the center and placed there a precarious pot of gum and cacao. María Teresa inspected the young girls and boys who needed their toenails trimmed. Doña María prepared a small gourd of *achiote* to paint the nails red. Several properly raised children offered themselves for the divination, but nearly all had a problem: a cracked toenail, only three long nails, pitch-black nails. But, by the hour of sunset, there were toenails found. Doña María painted only the girl's nails red, then placed both sets into a small cotton bag.

On the hour, Juan Aguacero waited upon a straw mat beside the fire and pot. Raúl was carried in on his throne of Lord of Festival.

"Now shut up!" Juan Aguacero said. "If you make a noise, I will stop."

He pulled an ocarina from within the folds of his shirt and slowly played a music that caused the spectators to put their hands over their ears and stare at one another with pinched faces.

"Now," Juan Aguacero said, his hands raised above his head, "to first find the problem, one must admit that there is a problem. And to make one such as Raúl admit that there is a problem will take some doing. Don't expect him to simply come out and say 'Yes, I will tell you that something is wrong with me. I was only playing, but now I see that it has all gone too far.' No, he won't do it! Only I, Juan Aguacero, can trick this Lord of Good Life. Only I can trick him into admitting to us all what is happening, and to admit it to himself. That is the most difficult of things."

He played the ocarina again; the villagers screwed up their faces. He finished and put the instrument away in his shirt. He then untied a string belt from around his waist and opened the leather pouch that hung from it. The magician sprinkled a red powder over his blackened feet and up his outstretched legs.

"I shame the red members of monkeys," Juan said. He waved his fingers over his legs, then knelt toward the pot. "I am Kavek of monkeys," he exclaimed. "I can coax the music from the world. I am Master of Artisans, those monkeys of our life."

Juan Aguacero then took the cloth of toenails and waved it over the pot of gum and cacao. The boiling liquid smelled of tar and smoked like rubber. "Only the dead will know which toenails are for them."

He turned toward Raúl and shook the bag as if meaning to throw it into the other's face. "You will be fooled!" The magician knelt by Raúl's feet and removed the gold painted sandals of the Lord of Festival. "A truly dead man," Juan Aguacero said, "needs all his nails to climb the world tree."

He took his knife and trimmed each of Raúl's thick toenails. As he cut, he spoke to the others. "He cannot find the replacements unless he is truly dead. Take his toenails and burn them. He must find the boy's nails, which are stronger, so that he can climb without faltering. If he falls, the earth will open and hold him forever in Xibalbá. He will fall and live with the Lords of Hell and their minions of pots and *metates*. Place his nails in the liquid. Push them down with a stick so if he tries to get them back he will burn his flesh. You are doomed, Raúl Cáscara, Good Life Deceiver!"

María Teresa did as the magician ordered. The smoke thickened and turned white as the nails burned.

Juan Aguacero took the bag of toenails and placed it by the pot. "Bring me water," he said.

He extinguished the flames, then chanted as the doused fire died and ascended the sky in defeated threads of smoke. The magician poured the remaining water onto the mixture of gum and cacao. Juan Aguacero fanned the thin wisps of steam appearing like cirrus clouds on the dusky liquid, then chanted words no others understood.

"Now," he said finally, "we shall all know that you are pretending, Raúl Cáscara. And that will open your lips."

And so, the magician threw the bag of toenails into the water. As the bag splashed, Juan Aguacero shouted with such suddenness and force that many in the circle recoiled in fright. "We shall see! We shall see!"

The magician danced around Raúl's body, repeating that Raúl would falter on the tree of death and fall to his eternal ruin. "Find your salvation!" Juan Aguacero commanded. He turned to the pot and snipped open the bag. Everyone noticed the surprise on the magician's face as he saw only unpainted nails floating.

"He has picked correctly! How can it be?"

The magician fished out the bag and stirred the toenails with a stick. "He won't be able to do it again," he said, then threw the bag back into the water. He waited several seconds before re-opening the bag. Once more, the unpainted nails floated above the painted nails.

The magician stood immobile. Dumbfounded. A trap-stick. "He is truly dead," he said. "This man is not pretending. He is dead. Dead!"

Raúl's friends gasped: at once feeling the sorrow of losing a loved one and at once feeling the bewilderment that denies recognizable emotion. How could he be dead and not rot away like the carcass he was? He was thinner—that no one could deny—but he was not putrid.

"There is something else here," the magician said, knowing full well the question in everyone's mind. "Something that needs more study." He stood as straight as his old body would allow and put both his hands up to his face in thought. "Bring me water from the Cunumán river," he said between fingers. "Get it where he was found. Bring me twenty *tzité* beans and dried corn husks. Bring me *cuxa* to drink and a cigarette to smoke. I will make the dead talk!"

Once more elaborate gestures were made over magical paraphernalia, once more chanting and taunting to discover the truth from Raúl. Only this time, with the rumor of the death of the Lord of Festival, the crowd surrounding Juan Aguacero grew to include everyone in the village. Other diviners and shamans pushed their way forward to shout suggestions. Of course, there was disagreement among these portentous minds all in a language of a secretive kind that swarmed above their heads like an effusion of gnats. The uninitiated were stupefied by the unintelligible language and the bantering of common words with elusive meanings. It seemed an impossible stew of wizardry.

Finally, with a great show of conviction, Juan Aguacero announced his findings:

"Raúl Cáscara," he said oratorically, "is dead!"

There came a great deal of coughing and harumphing among the other mystics.

"He is not rotting," Juan Aguacero continued, "because of the river he died in. The river and the blood of the warbling fig have made a gourd of Raúl. He is mummified into a husk. He has been punished for all his fakery, for not being faithful to himself. For pretending to be everything but his true nature, he has been killed and not killed. But I have found inside him the name that rattles there, the name that will release him from this neither-death-nor-life. He has been frozen with this name that clanks and rattles inside him like the nut of a dried mango. It is the name To-Bend-Word. This will be his release. In this place he will untie the knot of his fakery."

Juan Aguacero took out his knife and carefully pushed the point through the skin of Raúl Cáscara's chest. The escaping air was like the escaping air never mentioned by polite people. And in the sound of it, Juan Aguacero found the true name of the place To-Bend-Word. *Klou-wer*, it said.

"He has released the name of his release," the magician said. "He must be taken to Klouwer town."

And with Juan Aguacero's proclamation, there was general agreement. It was a disgrace to have neither-dead-nor-alive persons hanging around the village, but more than that, it was the duty of Raúl's friends and of the participants of the festival to save their Lord. No one would be accused of dishonoring the Lord of Festival just as no one would be accused of letting ghosts and half dead people wander aimlessly about his village. And certainly, no one would be accused of denying peace to a comrade and relative.

"How will we know where this place, Klouwer Town, is?" Diego Tzunún asked.

"It is in the north of the United States," Juan Aguacero declared.

That name held so much awe for the people of Motagua that they were silent for a very long time. They looked at one another and knew the seriousness and the mysteriousness filling each of their living shells like the stones of existence compressed in the flesh of mountains. K'ux Kah, Heart of Heaven, had only to say the names of things in order for them to be. It was in this way that the name, *United States*, filled them and became real and heavy within their bodies. Normally, knowing the name of a thing earned power over it, but here knowing the name "United States" instead subdued the knowers and gave power to the name itself.

In their silence, people from neighboring villages slid away from the center. Children clutched the hands of their parents and pulled homeward. The silence under the weight of "United States" worked against those not directly associated with Raúl. Their bodies were eased outward, forced to move quietly away, and to leave the skull of responsibility with those closest to Raúl. And after silence cleared the arena only Diego Tzunún, María Teresa, Chirón, Séptimo Tzuí and the youngest son of Doña María, Tecún Umán, were left with the shell of Raúl.

"It is our province," María Teresa said.

II

So they left. After Tecún Umán, leaving home for the first time, received the blessing of his mother and father, older brothers and sisters, cousins, priest, and friends, and received pieces of flesh from slaughtered animals—the triangular ears of pigs, the lean top skin of goats, the hoof of a bull, the hide of a calf, the flap of forehead from a goat all to protect the hearing and skin and mind and feet of him who goes out into the world for the first time—and, too, skin from other animals, representing the flesh which must be tanned and coarsened through the journey of life, received, also, herbs to ward off the general malaise of spirit, pine branches to burn in offering to Tazol, a gourd of coagulated pig's blood to spill on the slope of the first hill of the trek, and, of course, received his blanket packed by his mother, Doña María, with fishing line, bobbers, hooks, knives, scalers, rope, beef jerky, one change of clothes, hard candy from his youngest sister who looked upon him as the virile savior of humankind; and after Séptimo Tzuí hurried the training of his two sons so that they would care for the cemetery, the burials, medical operations, necropsies—which he did with them by practicing with chickens and piglets, day and night, every step from the observation of illness, to cutting flesh, to setting bones, to dissection, to the wake, to burial, to ritual mourning—wrote detailed and lengthy instructions for the distribution of responsibility while he was away and family wealth if he should not return, gave his wife the uninhibited passion of his love, making her the envy of all the women in the village, particularly those within hearing of the night cries, and his wife packed flint pieces, an ivory crucifix, clothes, food; and after María Teresa, having packed with her mother pots, pans, twine, cooking utensils, spices, four prayers to ward off pregnancy and evil men, clothes, having sworn faithfulness to the Virgin Mary, burned wax and pine needles in the cave alcoves, was blessed by her father, who consigned her to God, Raúl Cáscara—her be-loved—and to the others in the troop, and after she spoke with her mother in private so that those things between a mother and daughter would be cached within that eternal trove of female communion, and, with her family, walked into church with head covered and perfumed to incline in confession and to suck the wafer with eyes closed; after Chirón packed his flute and ledger and pen, his medallion of obsidian which warded off snakes, and his clothes and hunting gear, worked longer hours in the fields of Cusco Varado so that he could take money with him, planted in the corner of his house two stalks of corn and drew a wide circle around them, filling the rut with white stone from the Cunumán river, said good-bye to his family and the deaf girl, Jacinta, whom he loved dearly, rubbed oil in the wood of his doorway so that the souls of hunted birds would find shelter in his rafters; after Diego Tzunún, who from severe grief at the loss of his best friend, Raúl, lay face down in the dirt alongside his house for two days—drinking water and juice from gourds held by his wife, Elena, eating slivers of lime and coconut meat—and then bundled his clothes and wrapped food, tools, money, silver to trade, all in a blanket, blessed his young family and lay with his wife, both knowing that honor forbade him to return without having placed Raúl in the unknown Klouwer Town, dried his tears and kissed the eyes of his wife, then of his children; after the five friends dressed the hollow, rattling body of Raúl in his best clothes, bundled the most treasured of his belongings in silk, laced oxhide sandals onto his feet, trimmed his hair and beard, rubbed shavings from copper coins onto his eyelids, burned incense and cacao so that the smoke curled about Raúl, placed him on a wood frame so that he would not move or fall unless the carriers fell, asked his family for strength and forgiveness; after the village gathered together in an ominous shroud, huddling together like young rabbits as their prayers filled the air like rain, then helped carry the slender body of Raúl to the first hill where pig blood was poured out and more incense burned, and all shouted out their heartfelt love and respect for the six pilgrims, kissed and hugged the travelers, spoke softly, tearfully, wept, and admired the unfathomable faces of God; and after other things too numerous to mention here, they left.

Each understood that, compared to leaving, the journey would be a voyage through stone.

So then, following Juan Aguacero's general directions, signaled by a wave of his hand, the small band of pilgrims walked northward toward the mythic land of United States. They walked and took turns carrying Raúl. If one of the four carriers grew tired, the fifth person would be rotated. They walked through the ravines and woods of punished beasts, by-passing the large cities of Guatemala so that the forces of decadence and disbelief would not corrupt them and keep them from their quest. Juan Aguacero had warned them of the powerful forces of cities, so that they stopped only in small villages or *aldeas*.

Working for their food as they went, they kept that store which they had brought with them. Chirón, with his storytelling, recounted the situation with their Lord of Festival and of their pilgrimage to liberate his spirit. And, like a mailman, he took from each village some piece of information to pass on to the next, or some new and interesting story to earn shelter or food. Séptimo helped them earn by practicing medicine when needed, once even helping with a birth. Tecún Umán labored with his body, and so found work in every place they stopped. In exchange, the travelers received food, shelter and careful directions on how to avoid cities, how to circumvent the pervasive armies and police who demanded signatures and seals to walk on the earth, photographs and affidavits to follow the edge of a forest, and validation to step wherever it pleased a person to step.

It was young Tecún Umán, who questioned this openly: "It seems, does it not, that this business of papers and documents and permission to walk really finishes everything for people?"

Just in leaving Guatemala, they encountered the people of Cakchiquel, Mam, Solomeco, Jacaltec, Kanjobal, Ixil, Aguacatec, Tzutujil, Kekchí. And just over the Mexican border, in Chiapas, they encountered the Chicomuceltec, Chuj, Tojolabal, Tzeltel, Tzotzil, Chol and Chontal. The Maya world did not recognize the same border as Guatemala and Mexico, so in Chiapas they found echoes of their own world, echoes of an ancient walk from Zuyua of the seven caves. The five pilgrims and their Lord of Festival went undisturbed through the jungle valleys of Guatemala and across the border to the state of Chiapas and further into the states of Veracruz, Oaxaca, Puebla, Tlaxcala, Hidalgo, Queretaro, Guanajuato, San Luis Potosí, Zacatecas, and finally Coahuila before reaching the Mexican-Texan border. They encountered members of groups that comprised the hundreds of native peoples between Motagua and Texas. They met people and customs as varied as the Taracatians and the Icaiche, Toquegua and Comanche.

And throughout this journey—that would enlighten any people for all its history—María Teresa mothered the travelers and saved them from the anguish of solitude and alienation that often besets men. She did this so well that, upon nearing Texas, she immediately took charge in the northern states, and blazed a trail through the barren lands. She stopped, finally, at a juncture of two creeks in a scrub-filled ravine

"When the earth makes a sign of the womb," María Teresa said, "there can only be safety."

The men agreed and waited for her to lead them.

"Come on," she said, indicating the lights to the west. "We will find help there."

The town she led them to had only twenty buildings, all neatly in a double row. Lights strung along the eaves and strung between houses lit only the unpaved avenue so that darkness spread behind the buildings in a sea of dirt, dust and brush. The inside house lights were extinguished in all but one building. There, men and a few women sang on the raised porch of what appeared to be a *cantina*. The women were dressed in sleeveless blouses and tight skirts, and screeched like birds when pulling away from the rough clutches of the men. Yet only a few of the men in the center toyed with the women. Others merely joined the laughter while leaning back against the railings. One man, dressed in chaps and sombrero, plucked the strings of a guitar as if trying to discover what they were made of. The women flirted, got drinks for the men, then flirted again at the edges of inebriated fingers. All in all, there were some twenty people that grew in distinctiveness as the travelers warily approached. The travelers saw no children nor signs of family life, nor even of means of living except for the saloon.

They pulled tighter into the light of the street, instantly alerting the revelers. A large seated man gulped down his drink, then slapped the behind of a light-skinned woman. She and the other women hurried into the house. The man with the guitar slid the instrument around his back and pushed his sombrero up from his brow. The others cradled their drinks and watched with interest as the newcomers approached through the illumined night like apparitions through mist.

"Hello," María Teresa called out. There was no response. "Hello," she said, waving. "We have come a long way. We are searching for Klouwer Town."

The men against the rails looked at one another. The large man spoke in a slow resonant voice. "Well, this is Door of Sorrow," he said, lifting his index finger.

Above the man, etched into a gray plank of wood, was the name *Puerta Triste*.

"Have you heard of Klouwer Town?" Chirón asked.

"No."

"It is in the north of United States," Tecún Umán said.

The large man smiled. "Well, cutey, we know where the United States is." The other men laughed.

"It's big," the man added.

"If you help us find our way closer to Klouwer Town," María Teresa said, "we can do work for you and repay your kindness."

The men on the porch drew closer together.

"What do you have in mind?" the large man asked.

"I can do manual labor," Tecún Umán said. "Chirón is the best storyteller in Guatemala—"

"You're from Guatemala?" the guitar player asked.

"Yes," Diego answered. "We've come this way to help our Lord of Festival." Diego indicated the body of Raúl.

"He's a quiet one," the guitar player said.

"His spirit is not well. That's why we've come this far and traveled this long."

"And you need to go into the United States to find this Klouwer Town?" the large man wondered.

"Yes," answered María Teresa.

"Well, I've heard stranger reasons for wanting to go to the States. What makes you think we can help you?"

María Teresa stepped closer. "We're near, are we not?"

"Very," the large man said.

"We will gladly work for help and food. Or we can pay you for both."

The large man smiled again. "It seems that more and more are coming from Guatemala. From what part are you?"

"Motagua," Séptimo said.

"I don't know it." The large man turned to peer sidelong at the others on the porch. "Do any of you?"

The men shook their heads.

"It's a long way to Guatemala," the man said.

María Teresa reached the first step of the porch. "We've met many people and have worked for many people. Always, we've been shown kindness. The gods are very kind to poor travelers like us."

The large man smiled with one side of his mouth. "The gods are great," he said. "The gods are great."

"And kind," Séptimo added.

"There are some things I'll never know," the man answered. He stood and called out for a woman named Rosita. She came with a beer for him. "One thing I do know, though, is where the United States is. There are a great many who pass through, looking for the United States. Most of them don't care what city they get to. Some do, with families, but most just want to work. The United States is very rich. The richest in the world. But we're a poor town. We never see what becomes of the people who leave for money."

"We want to help our friend only," Diego said.

"Of course." The man turned the bottle of beer upward and drank with deep bubbling swallows. "They say that one can make enough money in a week to live for a year in Mexico. In the north—Chicago, New York, Gary, these are names I know. I've seen them."

Tecún Umán crossed his arms impatiently.

"Not everyone," the man said to Tecún Umán, "has friends to motivate him. The people who cross through here have many other reasons for going. Some aren't so good. Some are very good. And not all of them make it to where they want to go. It's not like here, where poverty is a disguise for you, a pair of sandals that everyone wears. Those who come back understand perfectly the depths of their poverty. Don't think it will be easy. You'll learn to hate yourself up in the United States."

Tecún Umán said defiantly, "We will pay for help."

"Do you speak English?" the man asked in English. When he saw the look of confusion, he asked again in Spanish.

"No," María Teresa said.

The large man turned to the guitar player and they spoke in English. The others spoke occasionally too, as if discussing what things could be done with the travelers. The men laughed at one point, then the large man spoke to the five pilgrims.

"Come and sit," he said. "Drink with us. You must be hungry." He ordered one of the women to bring food and beer. "Let's hear just a little more about you before we help."

The man with the guitar slid a chair closer to the large man. He turned the seat backwards and crossed his arms over the back. "And tell us why your Lord of Festival seems more dead than alive."

Chirón explained Raúl Cáscara's great ability to fake things, about the discovery of his body by the salt river and how Raúl held the vine of the warbling fig in one hand while both his feet were submerged. He explained how Raúl's body was galvanized by the gods of Motagua, his spirit dried like a bean within and made to rattle with the name of Klouwer. Chirón told them how Juan Aguacero discovered all this through his incantations and divinations, and how they followed his directions through Guatemala and Mexico. They were sure the gods of Motagua would lead them, with the help of others, unerringly to Klouwer Town. Their cause was just and unselfish.

As Chirón explained, the men of the narrow village inspected Raúl. They were unable to believe what they saw. They could not allow the idea that a dead man could remain as he was without putrefication. The men touched Raúl's body, felt along his nose and mouth to catch a hint of breath, but all they felt was the coldness and slightness of death. One man pried open the Lord of Festival's eyelids and closed them with a gasp when he saw the disturbed obsidian of the pupils. The men could not fit this limbo and this band of travelers into their vision of the world, and they became afraid.

"You act," María Teresa said, "unlike any Mexicans we've met."

"We live close to the border," the guitar player explained.

"Then this is a true border."

"It has a long history," the large man said, his voice more subdued, more full of justification, than it had been before Chirón's descriptions. "There are people living along here who prey on travelers like you. They can seem very friendly, but they gain a certain kind of meaning, of identity, by hurting others. Pain is their money."

The men looked up at their leader.

"We will help you," the man said, his eyes fixed on the body of Raúl Cáscara. "My name is Guerrero. This," he said while pointing to the guitar player, "is Luís Alfonso. The others are comrades."

The other men nodded. Two or three rose to shake hands with the travelers.

"Thank you," María Teresa said.

"We can only get you across," Guerrero said. "We can show you a map, but I don't share your faith that you'll find Klouwer Town."

María Teresa nodded.

Guerrero looked at her and spoke slowly, pointedly. "There are times when failure on the surface is actually success."

"What do you mean?"

He reached out as if welcoming her onto the porch again. "I say that to all who cross this border. Words to soften loss."

So, they planned late into the night—nearly to dawn—on how to get across the border and what kind of payment was to be given. The juncture of the Rio Grande and the Pecos River was decided upon as the most secure crossing point. From there, they were on their own. As payment, the travelers would clean every house in the village. Guerrero explained that the houses were not for the men on the porch, but for families that came to cross into the United States. Because of politics or increased vigilance by the Rangers, the whole village would sometimes be filled with waiting families. Then, Guerrero said, the town would seem to his men like their own villages, now so distant, and everyone would be happy. But when the houses were empty, as now, the men became sullen and prone to act badly.

"You are lucky," Guerrero said at the end of the evening.

The men of the village slept late into the next afternoon. It was this that finally convinced the pilgrims that here were people well able to help them, people who knew the United States.

María Teresa started early by washing linens and curtains in the creek. Diego and the others scrubbed walls and fixed broken slats in porches. They swept. Dusted.

Several men from the village left and did not return until past nightfall. They brought information on the chances for crossing the border. The chances were good for that night, but better for the following night.

"We'll wait for tomorrow," María Teresa said simply.

"No," Diego said. He spread his fingers. "If the chances are good, we should hurry. For Raúl's sake we should go tonight. What do the rest of you think?"

Chirón agreed with María Teresa, Tecún Umán with Diego.

"There is nothing without a little danger," Tecún Umán said.

"We should try to make it as little as possible," Chirón countered.

Séptimo turned to Guerrero. "Are the chances good or should we wait for tomorrow?"

"The chances are good and you can wait for tomorrow."

"Let's draw stones," Séptimo said.

They agreed. The stone for the first night was drawn from Guerrero's fists.

"So it is," Luis Alfonso said.

They waited until the mist around the juncture of the two rivers thickened and settled like a great bull afield. Guerrero swore he could lick the dense fog around the bank and find whether or not it was safe. That was what the pilgrims had paid him to do: place them at the edge of swimming with an arm in the air for directions, and a flick of the tongue to ignite their motion.

"God keep you," Guerrero said.

The cold water exhilarated them.

"Silent as a water snake," Guerrero advised. "Keep twenty feet out until the lake. You'll travel far. Northern shore to Devils River."

The travelers' dark skins hid them in the water.

"United States!" Tecún Umán shouted out, already concealed by the fog.

III

All that could be heard was a gentle lapping of water and the barking of bullfrogs. The dense air pressed the sounds of insects into a horizontal plane between fog and water. The travelers had long since quit speaking, and now pushed along at the depth of their chins. Now and then, a splash from a sudden drop-off arose like the leap of bass.

They followed the Rio Grande to a body of water called Amistad, then pushed along to find the mouth of Devils River. They had not expected the traveling to be so difficult or the voyage to be so long. They reached Amistad with the faintest signs of dawn. Not even the first dawn.

"The further past the river we get," Séptimo whispered, "the better our chances of not being found."

Their strength was ebbing with the weight of their clothes. María Teresa had first tied her skirt around her waist, the others had simply waded in, but it didn't matter with the water at their necks. Raúl floated in his carriage as a Lord on his raft, snake-bound, with a promise to return.

Further northward on the lake, they climbed ashore to rest in a niche of tall grasses. The bank sloped upward to a flat field and trees beyond. Not a person nor house was visible anywhere. Unlacing Raúl from the chair, they laid him down on the grass. María Teresa brought down her skirts and within minutes they all fell into a pitch-black sleep.

They awoke to a group of young men with rifles standing over them, shouting drunkenly in English and gesturing menacingly.

María Teresa tried to speak, but a fat boy raised a fist as if to hit her. "Damn wetbacks," the boy said.

There were seven of them, the eldest being just over twenty years old. The youngest, a gangly boy of seventeen, leaned against a truck parked above the bank. He wavered as though nauseatedly drunk. The smell of alcohol was strong.

When the five travelers stood, a tall boy—the eldest—pointed at Raúl's body then jerked his chin at Diego Tzunún.

"Get him up," he said.

Diego understood the gesture and tried to explain that Raúl could not stand.

"They don't speak English," the fat boy said, spitting.

The tall one kicked at Raúl's side. Diego moved quickly to stop him, but the boy smashed Diego's ribs with the rifle butt. Diego collapsed as the boy spun awkwardly to aim at Tecún Umán and the others before they could move to defend themselves.

"Don't move a goddamn finger," he shouted. "Check that one dude out, Tom."

The fat boy moved beside Raúl. He pushed the body. He lifted Raúl's head by grasping the hair, then let the head drop with a thud. "He's dead."

The other boys standing on the bank stepped closer. The boy by the truck didn't move.

"You suppose they killed him?" one of them asked.

"I don't know," the tall one said. "These people are likely as not to do anything."

"Maybe they was just going to bury him, Jim," another boy said.

"Naw, they're all wet. They wouldn't be burying him wet. Something's up with them."

Tom walked up the slight incline, wheezing from exertion and drinking. "They was probably going to throw him in and let the fish eat him."

"Ask for their papers," a boy said. "I know they don't got none."

"I don't have to ask nothing," Jim said. "You can tell by looking at 'em they don't got papers."

"They in trouble for sure," Tom said. "We could shoot 'em right here and now and nobody'd say shit."

"Hell yeah!" one of the others said. "The way people's complaining about the jobs going to wetbacks, nobody'd care. Let's shoot their asses. Fuck 'em! Bastard Spicks!"

One of the boys pointed to Raúl's body. "With this dude dead like he is, everybody'd think they killed him and then turned on each other."

"Look at 'em," Jim said, "They don't even know the trouble they found."

"They think they can come in and do anything they damn please," the other boy continued. "If we don't shoot 'em, Jim, then we oughta at least beat hell out of 'em."

The other boys joined in, half frightened and half excited by their brave talk.

"Too bad the girl's ugly," Jim said.

The others chortled grotesquely. The boy by the truck tried to laugh, but he moaned instead and held his head.

"Ol' Delbert ain't going to make it," said Tom.

"Let's give the girl to Delbert," another said.

The boys laughed lewdly then, and stared at María Teresa. Without understanding any of their words, she felt what they were thinking. Diego lay clutching his chest. Séptimo, Chirón and Tecún Umán moved protectively toward María Teresa.

"What do they want from us?" Tecún Umán said.

The boys pointed their rifles at Tecún Umán. One of them spat on the ground close to his feet.

"Please," Chirón said, his hands slowly lowering.

"He's saying please. That's what 'por favor' is."

Chirón looked at Diego, then at Jim. "Please," he said again.

Jim motioned with the rifle for Chirón to get close to Diego.

"Get me the bottle," Jim ordered.

A boy stepped up and reached out with it. Jim took a gulp, then handed it to Tom.

"His ribs are broken," Chirón said.

María Teresa moved toward Diego. Tom shouted at her, threatening her again with his fist. The travelers remained still.

"That's the way with these greasers," Tom said. "They like their men to beat the fuck out of 'em. Makes 'em horny."

The boy by the truck vomited, then gagged repeatedly. The boys on the bank laughed too loudly.

"Wonder what makes Delbert horny?" one said to Jim.

"Leave him alone. He's just a boy."

"I told you he shouldn't have come," the one continued.

"Shut up," Jim yelled. "You don't tell me nothing, you hear? Nothing!"

"Man," said Tom, "Let's get out of here." He looked at Jim.

"Sure, sure. But first we got to teach these grease balls a lesson. You guys take the girl up by Delbert."

Four boys moved down the slope and reached for María Teresa. They laughed as she tried pulling away. Tecún Umán grabbed at one, but Tom lashed out with the rifle butt. The crack of Tecún Umán's collar freed a shriek of pain from him. The other boy kicked Tecún Umán into the water, where he fought to keep his footing. He lay half in the water and half out, writhing in pain. Instantly, the boys lunged at Séptimo and Chirón. The older men defended themselves feebly, and were quickly knocked down to the water. Their faces were torn, their mouths bleeding. Séptimo lost consciousness.

María Teresa tried to slap free of the boys holding her, but they quickly held her arms behind her back. Tom, laughing viciously, tore at her clothes until she stood naked except for sandals and underclothing.

"She's an old hag," Tom said.

The boys pushed her down by the truck. Delbert stood over her, trying to control his stomach, trying not to look at her.

"Come on, Delbert," Tom said, "you got yourself a woman now."

Another boy pushed Delbert on top of María Teresa. She screamed and struggled beneath the boy. Delbert vomited again, partly on her chest.

"Oh fuck," Jim said.

Tom turned to keep from vomiting.

Jim reached down and pulled Delbert off María Teresa. One of the boys poured the remaining whiskey onto her. She scrambled to her knees, her eyes doe with fear. She stood to run, but Tom grabbed her and spun her back.

"Leave her alone," Jim commanded. "She's had enough."

But Tom reached between her legs and pushed a finger up against her. María Teresa screamed at him, twisted away, and ran through the grass by the water's edge.

The boys whistled and catcalled behind her. When she fell away from sight, the boys descended to throw the other travelers into the lake. Tecún Umán and

Chirón grabbed at Séptimo to keep him from drowning. Diego splashed in the shallows and Raúl's body floated out like a log.

Reflexively, Jim raised his rifle to his shoulder and fired a shot into Raúl. The body spun like a coffee can, the name "Klouwer" clinking inside.

"This is what we came to do, boys," Jim said.

Another boy lifted his rifle and shot. The body spun out. Raúl's arms scooped up strands of seaweed. The boys shot again and again, each time sending the body spinning further away.

"The last one to hit him wins," Jim said.

The six boys on the bank lined up and took aim. Delbert lay by the truck watching. Each time a shot hit Raúl, Delbert closed his eyes. The spinning body brought back the vertigo of drunkenness, the smell of vomit, his humiliation.

The further away the body spun, the more the shots spit up water alongside Raúl. His body had so many nicks and strands of seaweed that he looked like a moss-covered log floating away. It wasn't long before Jim and Tom were the only two able to hit Raúl with regularity. The others conceded.

"Hell," Tom said after missing, "no wonder you can hit him. He's going out on your side."

"Like hell," Jim said. "Let's trade places and I say I still beat you."

The firing continued until Tom missed three times.

"Want to bet?" Jim asked.

"A dollar," Tom said.

Jim took steady aim, waiting for the suspense to build, then fired a single shot into Raúl. He stood back, smiling.

"I won."

"You're fucking lucky," Tom said, "that's all. Fucking lucky."

Jim laughed. "Yeah. Next time you'll be saying that it was because you was drunk."

The boys shoved and shouldered each other into the pickup. Already, they had allowed the images of the travelers to evaporate from their minds. Instead, they ridiculed Delbert and damned their lack of alcohol. One of the boys in the bed of the truck lifted his finger to his eye and fired a bead through the dust behind the truck and into the slowly revolving body of Raúl.

The travelers, separated and defeated, watched Raúl's body tumble away from them in the swells of the lake. They watched helplessly, more pained by the harsh realization of the impossibility of their pilgrimage than by their broken bones and torn skin. They saw the face of their naivete, their simplicity of vision, turn into sheer stupidity. Yet, with that self-hate lodged inside them, they saw their only success. The word "reality" had taken on such indelible twists and turns upon crossing the border—had become something that changed voice and style and meaning from Motagua to the fabled land of "United States"—that Klouwer Town was everywhere around them. It seemed to them, staring wide-eyed from the lake shallows, that all of the United States was a place of bending words.

As if to console them, Raúl's body was so entangled with seaweed, leaves, flecks of debris, that it became indistinguishable from the myriad other objects floating on the crosscurrents and rivulets, rising and falling in the slow lake-swells. And in this, the travelers knew the end of their pilgrimage. They had brought their Lord and friend, and had left him fully immersed in this vast Klouwer place. Only northward. Only fish-road, only swan-path north. Northward the waves took him, rafting solemnly on.

REMEMBERING

THE VANGUARD OF WOOD

▼

And then the gods spoke and said the truth: "These dolls of wood shall come out well. They will speak and converse over the face of the earth."

— Popol Vuh

Hah! Let me tell you just how the children of God went about in that early day:

K'ux Kah, Heart of Heaven, allowed wells and ignorance to fit side by side. In searching out the Quiché, he had made men of mud, but as mud will do, the men merely floundered. So wood was tried next. Don't ask why if you don't know! It was simply done under a liquid maroon sky, moonless and sunless, but still colorful, with distant volcanoes, deep valleys and verdurous hills. It was done there, under the will of Heart of Heaven, K'ux Kah. It was a formidable place by its potential alone!

At that time, it is said, people walked about nearly mute, digging roots from their fields like wooden effigies. But Don Felipe was the worst. His language was grunting or shouting in anger. His gestures to others were menacing ones. He lived alone on his *cerro* and thank god it was so, everyone said.

Up on his hill, in the one room hut, Don Felipe bellowed to himself like an anxious bull. Ceiba and her young friends stopped by the well and listened. They held each other's arms and turned up their faces.

"Furnace!" they exclaimed, which really meant nothing.

Like the others, the girls sometimes spoke without understanding what they said.

"We shall be turned into monkeys," one girl said.

"Hush and walk slow," said a passing man.

They listened by the well until the bellowing ended, then played as before beneath the lemon tree.

And so, under the crab nebula—close enough then to fondle, Ceiba often gazed skyward. On the slope of an adolescent hill, she would cradle the night in her fingers and crane her neck to ensure she was not seen, softly place her palm on the gentle slope of her breast and try to hum that sensual drone which always awakened her and always brought her to these very moments. The hummingbird of dreams had been coming more frequently to her sleep, but it always came enveloped in clouds or limping as if wounded.

It was difficult to know or see the dreams. The sound of surprise was there—a popping in the bird's tubular throat—and a certain nautical smell, like fish and cacao. But laced through each vague image was a viscous tone that both pleased and frightened her. It was as if the soft hum of adult secrets were lapping the shore of her dreams, promising something she could only guess at.

This guessing produced a fear much like the fear Ceiba and her friends experienced playing by the well when—sometimes after Don Felipe's wondrous bellowing—rabbits and jaguars loped together across the hills. They stretched their forelimbs out as if in supplication, patting the earth, then pulled their hindquarters up from behind. The hills were near enough and the number of pairs high enough, that the girls clearly saw the ancient enemies running together, as if conspiring by their closeness to frighten the girls. The girls certainly did not understand this.

In fact, this same uncertainty—and the ambiguity of all that surrounded them—imbued everything with imminence. Ceiba and her two friends, as did the others of the village, lived not by reason, but by imagery.

Ceiba, working at the *pila*, would pick up a bar of lye and gaze at it as if trying to unravel the impurities in the gypsum white. And her mother, Doña Cheni, would put her towel across her shoulders, look on her growing daughter, and speak.

"Get back to work! It's one thing to be running around like a blind peccary with your friends, but not when there's work to be done!"

"Yes, Mother."

Then, walking back to her own work—virtually exhausted from speaking so much—Doña Cheni would mutter, "There's nothing like puberty to send you packing."

Discussions like these so often drained them that they would work together for days afterward, preparing black beans and tortillas, or chile stew, and cleaning house without saying another word.

And every other day, Ceiba pressed the bar of lye into the family's clothes, then rubbed the clothes over the rippled stone of the *pila*. In this way, she cleaned the clothes and scraped the lime colored moss growing on the laundry rock. Both were interminable duties. The moss, like laundry, grew overnight and helped bring insects into the kitchen. The insects of the kitchen pond lured frogs, which brought snakes, which brought the iguanas with their scissor teeth.

"The beef of snakes," Ceiba said one day while working at the *pila*, "is cylindrical."

She immediately remembered her dreams, and their sensual drone that always awakened her just before discovering the source of it. Always there was the smell of the sea. Shells, it is said. She held the bar aloft and found the inner thigh of a tapir in the swirls.

"Oh, wonder," she thought, "wilt thou pan bread?"

Answers seemed never to come for any of the girls. Ceiba's mother would, at best, rub her lower lip between her fingers as if it were a thread of dough, and rarely say more than, "These things become less apparent as you grow older."

"Or they don't," Ceiba would say.

"Yes, of course."

Cucurbit, Ceiba's closest friend, also approached the same age, so that the two of them blushed together or rolled their shoulders in secretive shyness. Galethia, the youngest, still scintillated with innocence. But Galethia was the most visionary of the three. Her eyes were black like the others', except on the skirt of her irises, where red and green alternately dominated. Her small hands, the color of coconut, were nimble and incessantly active. Galethia was the one who motivated the three to play in trees or race mango hairs through the eyes of needles. She invariably won. And Galethia would suddenly speak as if in a trance and utter unintelligible comments such as "neutrinos have mass," "supersymmetry," or "coelacanth."

It was no great surprise, then, on a day when Ceiba and Cucurbit found it particularly difficult to look each other in the eyes because of their shyness, that Galethia spoke slowly and sadly.

"I see the hallway where you two stand," she said. "It will be the same hallway for me."

Ceiba rubbed her cheeks as if trying to erase her blush.

"Can you see everything?" asked Cucurbit, fearfully.

"Only the hollowing of wood, and its peculiar drone of ants."

Ceiba touched Galethia's elbow and leaned closer to her friend's ear. "Tell us more about the drone," she said. "Cucurbit and I both want to know. Right, Cucurbit?"

Cucurbit put her hand to her mouth and nodded.

"This same drone," Galethia said, "will be for me, too."

The other girls shrugged.

"The drone is mysterious," Galethia continued. "It floats between your navel and your knees. The back of your knees, not the front. It has the long smell of the sea. The tucking away of ancient waves, and the sigh of mollusks."

"And its origin?" asked Cucurbit.

"That's the thing I cannot see."

Ceiba stamped her foot. "You don't know any more than we do! Why are we listening to her?"

"In the manner of night," Galethia warned, "it will come to us."

"Mumbo jumbo!"

"Don't mock me, Ceiba!"

"Oh, all right," she said, "but let's quit talking about this."

Galethia shook herself, becoming suddenly aware that the inability to explain was just as uncomfortable for her as for the other two.

"Let's hang like gourds," she said.

The game was not usually very exciting—hanging from their knees on different levels of a tree—but they agreed. The trick was to climb as high as one dared, then to drop limply. The girls' skirts drooped down over their bodies and just covered their faces so that they looked more like closed magnolias than gourds. They hung quietly and contemplatively as proper gourds should, allowing the wind to shudder through the leaves and petals of their skirts. Better this, to be enveloped in the chrysalis shade of skirts, than to speak of things they couldn't understand.

They had hung for an hour when they heard the deep bellowing of Don Felipe. They said nothing, and hung even more convincingly as gourds. Nearly half an hour later, though, Ceiba spoke out in a hollow voice.

"My mother bleeds," she said.

The girls had emulated the sway of gourds so well that they shared a common consciousness just as gourds do. There was no need to explain what Ceiba meant. The understanding of it pooled in each of their minds.

They climbed down from the branches and stared in the direction of Don Felipe's hut.

"We must go home," said Ceiba.

Cucurbit blushed and nodded. "Goodbye," she said without looking into the faces of her two friends.

Galethia waited until Cucurbit was well out of earshot. "You are afraid," she said, then.

Ceiba shifted her arms.

"I am too. I know what you hear—"

"Oh, Galethia," Ceiba said. "You've already said that you didn't."

"But I know what you know."

Ceiba let her arms drop limply by her sides. "Let's just go home."

"But I don't want it to happen," said Galethia. "I don't want it ever to happen to me."

"What?"

"I think I can stop it. I can keep this change from coming."

"What change? And how?" Ceiba asked.

Galethia clamped her hands beneath her arms. "I don't know yet."

Ceiba laughed sharply.

"I mean, I'm not sure yet."

"Go home, Galethia!" Ceiba turned to walk away.

"Wait! Please." Galethia put her fingers on the older girl's elbow.

"What?"

"Can I kiss you? Hold you?"

Ceiba looked angrily for a moment, then softened. "Go home. We'll play tomorrow."

The next day, only the two older girls came out to play by the lemon trees. They waited for Galethia, but she never came.

That night, Ceiba tried an experiment in her bed. She lay very still on her back, her arms outstretched, and slowed her breathing until she controlled each shallow breath. She wanted her body to be pliable and tolerant. She had heard that the *Ah-kij* could leave her body and travel like a bird through the night. She had heard that it was a matter of making the body soft and content. And a matter of faith, but faith in *what* she did not know. It was as if by some strange conviction, one could stand against the body's separate will and learn the secrets behind shadows.

She lay very still. She heard a bird fly from a nearby tree. There was hope!

Ceiba concentrated on being immobile in bed, her thoughts jumping to Galethia and Galethia's strange eagerness to prevent the change. Galethia had wanted to kiss her. Could that, somehow, be connected to the change? Ceiba concentrated and allowed the vision of a screech owl to possess her mind. Don Felipe's scream filled the village. He was walking about.

Ceiba dismantled her owl. Don Felipe was an immense man, who seemed to always amble in a brackish mist. His legs were thick and muscular, his head too large for his body. And his body seemed always to move independently of his will. Even when he stood still, his body seemed to gurgle and ripple like a cat's lithe body. In Ceiba's mind, he always stood with hills behind him. A thick branch curved smoothly beside him.

A small animal scurried alongside the hut. Quietness squatted over the village, allowing only the distant tread of Don Felipe. He was walking about. She imagined him again: trampling bushes; snapping branches underfoot; cutting a swath through the village like some great beast, dumbly charging. His unintelligible shouts only served to strengthen Ceiba's image of him as a marauding animal.

It was an alluring sound in the otherwise sepulchral night. She arose from bed and peered through the branches of the wall. In each shadow of tree, she saw the amorphous hulk of Don Felipe. His heavy footfalls seemed now to come from here, then from over there. His shouts threaded ubiquitous through the air. Then, suddenly, the image of his smell came to her. She smelled that brief heat of a horse as it shifts its weight in sleep.

She turned this smell in her mind, seeing it from every angle, and failed to hear the footsteps coming close to her hut. Then like a horse she never saw, Don Felipe sniffed along the wall. She stepped back, her throat clutching her breath, her mind full of a carnivorous horse seeking its prey.

The barest sound escaped her, like a midnight coo of troubled sleep.

Don Felipe brushed against the wall, and the branches shuddered. He sniffed, walking more cautiously as he neared the area where Ceiba slept. He prodded the earth with his leaden feet, then stopped only a meter from Ceiba.

The darkness of the wall deepened where he stood. Ceiba clutched her hands, sure that he would rip apart the house and tear her life away. She dared not move.

His breathing came close, nestling between the branches like a nuzzling beast. Then, instead of the cruel voice she expected to hear, she heard Don Felipe whisper her name in the voice of melting icicles.

Even without being there, one knows she did not answer.

"Ceiba," he said again. "I know you are there, Ceiba."

Even if she had wanted to, she could not speak.

"Ceiba," he said. "Come close to me. Come close, Ceiba."

The night became a silent shrug of some vast bird.

"Come close and listen, Ceiba. I have come for you. I have come for you."

Don Felipe pushed a fingertip through the branches.

"Touch me," he said. "I have come to tell you the secret of your dreams. I know them."

Ceiba felt naked and ashamed of her body.

"Don't be afraid," he said. "I have come to help. I will not hurt you."

Ceiba could only shake her head.

"I've come to talk. I know your dreams and the source of all the droning of night."

"But why?" Ceiba tried to say. Her voice broke.

"In a million years," Don Felipe said, as if hearing her, "people will kill each other. Listen. The weight of the world rests on you."

"Bruit," Ceiba said.

"Come close and listen. You are a falcon growing wings. An unfertilized egg.

Come close to me. Feel my breath."

Ceiba listened to his rhythmic breathing, to the smoothness of his voice, and stepped forward.

"Listen to me," he said. "Can you hear the water lapping the smooth rocks of shore? Listen to the birds as they chatter to the sea. And the distant drone that approaches you. Do you hear the wind? The hiss of sea foam? The great lurching of whales? Ceiba, Ceiba. What is the name of God?"

"What?" she said.

"Tell me the name of God."

Ceiba felt her tears rising. "What do you want?" she said.

He laughed softly. "I want your promise."

"What do you want?" she asked again, the hysteria rising inside her.

"The promise of your will."

Ceiba stepped back.

"There are things you cannot dream of," he said. "There are Gods more frightening than I could ever be. They'll snap you up from the ground and pluck off your head like a grape. And they want us to love them. No, they demand it, Ceiba...in their secretive way. Silent tyrants!"

"Go away," she pleaded.

"They are so vile, Ceiba, that they have a million and one names. And you don't know one. They expect us to find their names—one name!—and worship to save our lives. Don't be like the rest, Ceiba. With me, there is only the pleasure of the sea in denying their name. Whale-song! Dolphin-hymns!"

A sob escaped from Ceiba.

"I will lead you to that drone you search for at night. I can show you the exquisite place of your dreams."

"Please go away," she said.

"Quiet your body. Yes, let your body forgive you."

"Please...what do you want?"

Don Felipe put his hand against the wall. "A new race of men! A new universe! I want a world that is free of these devils."

"Please," she said, fearing his rising voice.

"I want your soft thigh and the love of good will."

"I don't understand—"

"Sh!" he said. "I am the beast of your dreams. The keeper of your dreams.

And of your drone."

"No."

"The drone that makes you fragile. I know all about it. I know the tickle of your bones."

"Please go away..."

"Stop! I'll speak until I am finished. Or tear this wall down. Now, come closer."

Ceiba stood still.

"Tonight, you will know something of the world. Yes, Ceiba. Even though you do not join me, you will know."

Ceiba sobbed.

"Put your face against the branches," he said. "Do it slowly and quietly or all the power of evil will ravage your heart."

"No—"

"Do it!"

Ceiba leaned forward so her forehead touched the branches. She felt her tears run from her eyes, and the heat of his body only a short distance from her face.

"Now listen," he said. "Listen to me carefully."

His face came close to hers, so that his whisper filled her ears and mouth.

"You will put your hands against the wall," he said. "You will put them above your head."

Ceiba did not move.

"Do it, my child. Or die!"

She did as she was told, the fear swelling inside her as if blown from the heat of his breath.

"Now," he said, his voice low before her. "Open your mouth. Open."

Tearfully, Ceiba opened her mouth.

Don Felipe leaned nearer, his face directly in front of hers. "Do exactly as I tell you."

Ceiba closed her eyes.

"Breathe deeply," he said. "Breathe deeply, and slowly."

Ceiba swallowed her fear as his breathing came slowly and hotly through the branches.

"Breathe," he repeated. "Sweet breathing..."

Ceiba did as he ordered, feeling her own breath matching his so that in that sharing of air, her fear began dissolving away.

"Slowly," he said. "Slowly…"

And in that sharing, she heard the hummingbird's warble, and she recognized a new weight in her abdomen.

"Steady," Don Felipe said. "Breathe and recall that tone of your dreams."

They shared the air inside them until that strange commingling heightened her awareness of her own body. She breathed as if hypnotized, breathing his hot breath deep into her lungs, then giving her own back to him in a slow rhythm that seemed to solidify the air passing back and forth.

The dark inside of her mind was full of the sea.

"Now," he said, pulling back slowly, "go to bed. Find the secret of your body."

Ceiba stood against the wall as he turned away. She leaned against the wood even as he lumbered off. She peered between the branches, full of the image of his moving body, his muscles tensing and relaxing, the strength of his legs.

The next day, Ceiba worked more distractedly than ever. Doña Cheni scolded her, but nothing changed. The visitation seemed a dream to her: unreal except as the most haunting of dreams. But as such, it colored everything she did. She wanted to run and tell Cucurbit, tell her that she had found the source of the sound, that there was light and sadness there. But when Ceiba went, after chores, to the lemon trees where Cucurbit played alone, she could not bring herself to speak upon seeing Cucurbit's bashful face.

The following day, then, it was Cucurbit who came running headlong toward Ceiba, and clutched Ceiba's arm until it left marks. Their exuberance in meeting—the brightness of their faces—revealed everything. They quaked with that awareness, gyrating and oblivious to everything around them.

Galethia's voice came down from above. "You have seen Don Felipe."

Ceiba and Cucurbit looked up in surprise. They had thought themselves alone. Galethia hung by her knees from a branch, her small face peering down from within the cup of her skirts.

"Where have you been?" Cucurbit demanded.

"How do you know we saw him?" Ceiba asked.

"He told me he would see you."

"When?" Cucurbit asked.

"He came to my house three nights ago."

"But you're the youngest," said Cucurbit.

"He said that I wasn't ready for him, yet, but that we were allies. I will never be ready for him. Or any man. I know the way to stop this."

"We don't want to stop this," Ceiba said.

The two older girls looked at each other and giggled. Galethia stared down from within her skirts.

"How will you stop it?" Ceiba asked defiantly, holding Cucurbit's arm.

"Have you ever wanted the red flower?"

"What are you talking about?" Cucurbit asked.

"The way you dreamed of Don Felipe. With the drone of your dreams filling your fingers, and your mouth overflowing with flowers. Have you ever wanted to touch a woman?"

"You're talking gibberish," Ceiba said.

"This is the way to stop the dreams. Don Felipe showed me that. We are allies."

Ceiba shifted uncomfortably. "What are you talking about?"

"I want the love of women, not of men."

The older girls looked up at Galethia as if she were an enormous aphid sucking the life from trees.

"What is the world coming to?" Cucurbit asked.

"You're obscene," said Ceiba, spitting to remove the taste of the idea.

"No, you're wrong. I see the slate succumbing in folds on the river bottom."

"She's crazy!" Cucurbit said.

"The hate of gods," Galethia continued. "A world that could have been, instead of this one."

"Get away from us," Ceiba said.

"And the end of the world because of forgetfulness."

"She talks just like him," Cucurbit said.

"He and I are allies. Against the evil of gods. Turn away and die with virtue. Dignity is better than worship of whim."

"Let's go," Ceiba said, pulling at Cucurbit.

"Idiot!" Cucurbit shouted up.

The older girls left as Galethia called to them from inside the tree. They turned to look back, but Galethia was lost in the leaves. Only her voice followed them down the hill.

"You are the foolish ones!" she shouted. "Tomorrow, you'll see! The end approaches. Repent unto your will! Find conviction! Welcome your soul within yourself. Slander those who would work you up from mud and wood. Do not bend! O, stupid ones! Do not bend! It is better to snap than bend. Tomorrow is the rain of glue!"

"She's a lunatic," Ceiba said.

"Unfit to breathe air," Cucurbit said.

The girls ran to their mothers and told what Galethia had said. Their mothers were dismayed: What things wicked were in the world that bred such vile creatures? They called together the other women of the village.

"This needs action," said Doña Cheni.

The women gathered and tried to recall or invent a way of dealing with the nastiness in their midst.

"There are terrible things afoot," a thin rail of a woman said.

She turned to Galethia's mother and demanded a response, but the frumpish woman said that she would abide by what the others wished.

"Soak her in salt water," said a fat woman. "That will draw out the poisons."

"Let's offer her to Don Felipe," Doña Cheni said.

"Yes," they all shouted. "That'll turn her head!"

"He will scour the evil."

And so, the women walked out in single file to find Galethia. They tracked her to the tree where the girls had left her. She still hung upside down, but now she smiled with the smile of one who knows her destiny.

"Come down from there!" the women called.

"I am the first martyr," Galethia answered. "Saint Galethia. They will name cities after me."

"Come down, or we'll chop the tree down!"

Galethia smiled and climbed slowly down, her face brilliant red from hanging for so long.

"Will you change your ways?" the woman asked.

"No."

"Tie her up," Doña Cheni commanded.

The women trussed her up like a captured goat and carried her to Don Felipe's hut on a long pole.

"Suffer for thy evil ways," the women said in chorus. "Repent and find the way of the mundane."

"Go to hell," Galethia said.

"My child," her mother said, "why are you doing this to me? What have I done to deserve this? Don't you love your mother? Don't you care about her? I've tried to be a good mother."

"You've been a good mother," she said, patting her hand, "but this is bigger than both of us. Don't take it personally."

Far above the ascending group, Don Felipe began his terrible bellowing. His yelling poured down the hill like so much gravel that the women had to hold up their hands to shield their faces. Galethia's mother bravely covered her daughter's body with her own.

They walked as far as they could, until the screams from above were unbearable upon their shoulders.

"Leave her here," a woman said, finally. "Let the horse find her."

They took Galethia down and bound her to a tree.

"Will you change your attitude?" asked Doña Cheni. "This is your last chance."

"Never!"

"But, daughter, my child, won't you see the error of your ways?"

Galethia shook her hair free. "There's a certain grace in living with principle."

"Will you repent?"

"This is your last chance," Galethia answered. "Give up your bovine ways. Learn the name of Him who oppresses you. Rebel against Him!"

"She's beyond help," her mother said. "Oh, where did I go wrong?"

"Imbeciles!" yelled Galethia. "Children of potted plants!"

The women returned down the hill, lingering like strands of saliva, hoping that Galethia would call them back. Instead, she cursed them.

"Flatulents!"

So, the wayward children of K'ux Kah, Heart of Heaven, waited into the evening for the sounds of conformity to rain down from the hill. If they had known how to pray, they would have. As it was, they huddled together like marmosets, sniffing and scratching at each other. Who's to say there wasn't a little jealousy among them?

But it wasn't the screams of conformity that they heard early the next morning. The sky had become resinous and the air smelled like tar. The screaming to them was a spectral horde cascading down the thickened air. The women held their hands to their mouths to keep from screaming back in fear.

"He's devouring her," Doña Cheni cried. "He mistook our offering."

"My daughter!" Galethia's mother screamed. "We must save her!"

They hurried up the hill, carried as much by an earnest desire to save Galethia, as by a crescendoing fear that gave them inertia. The screaming, too, crescendoed. Some of the older women stopped dead in their tracks, impaled by the gruesome noise as if by spits. The sky grew more and more resinous, as if those terrible screams were coated in Galethia's blood and had risen to coagulate in the brackish sky.

And upon reaching the hut, many of the women averted their eyes to keep from vomiting. The ground buckled underfoot. The fence danced and clattered its boards. Rocks leapfrogged by the door of the hut. More frightening yet was the torn body of Don Felipe. Forks and knives scurried over him like gamboling crabs, too involved to notice the shocked onlookers. A deep throated urn took large bites from his thighs and swallowed without chewing. Pots and pans nipped at his thick flesh, and a nutcracker snipped the joints of his fingers.

The women drew closer to find Galethia, but spatulas and tongs lunged at them in warning. Off to one side, and just behind a crazed mortar and pestle, Galethia squirmed in pain. Her body had been attacked and eaten, but she continued fighting a red clay stove.

Her mother snatched a thick stick from the ground and beat at the stove until it retreated into the fenced area.

"My poor baby," her mother said, her tears pouring forth. "What have I done?" She cradled Galethia's face in her arms.

"This is the end for all of us," Galethia whispered.

"Sh, sh," her mother said.

Galethia smiled. "It is the end, Mother. The world will destroy us all."

"No, don't talk like that—"

"Be brave, Mother. This is the way it will end: The sky will rain glue and everything of the world will destroy you. Rabbits and chairs will hunt you down. They are jealous of our chances."

Ceiba and Cucurbit approached.

"Is there no hope?" her mother said, rocking her daughter. "Is there no good?"

Galethia laughed and coughed blood.

"Ugh," Ceiba said.

"Yes. There is hope and good. But not for you." Her words came haltingly. "For you, there is only the commonplace. But, even for that, it is almost too late."

"Almost?"

Galethia tried to laugh again, but the sound choked her. "Call upon your god! Worship Him who has made you of wood. That's your salvation. Place your face into the mud of your ancestors—and serve!"

"What god?" Cucurbit asked fearfully.

She smiled ironically. "Ask Don Felipe."

"But he's dead," Ceiba said.

"God has a million and one names," Galethia answered. "All you need is one."

Galethia's mother began to cry. "Tell us the name," she pleaded.

"For a world of wooden cows?"

"Tell us!" Cucurbit demanded.

"Start with the A's."

"I hate you," Cucurbit said.

Ceiba shouted at Cucurbit. "Never mind! Start with A's!"

"Aaa," said Cucurbit.

Galethia laughed.

"Aab. Aac. Aad."

"What a moron," Galethia said.

Cucurbit turned savagely and kicked at Galethia. Something round and red shot from Galethia's mouth.

"Why did you do that?" screamed Ceiba, holding Cucurbit back by the arm. "She wouldn't have told us anyway!"

Galethia moaned and hacked, trying to regain her strength. She motioned with her fingers. "Ceiba," she whispered. "Ceiba."

Ceiba knelt beside Galethia and put her ear close. "What is it?"

"I just wanted to say." The words came with great difficulty. "To say, that,

that she would never reach the M's."

"M's!" Ceiba screamed back at Cucurbit. "Start with the M's!"

"Maa. Mab. Mac."

Galethia grinned, tried to laugh, then fell limp into the arms of her mother.

"My baby," her mother cried. "My poor baby."

"Mad," Cucurbit said. "Mae. Maf."

Ceiba joined Cucurbit: "Mag. Mah. Mai."

Galethia's mother turned her face away from her daughter. She lifted her face heavenward to join in the naming of god:

"Maj. Mak…"

Then the other women, too, turned up their faces and entered into the naming:

"Mal. Mam. Man…"

ALONG A WHITE ROAD NORTH

▼

B<small>LOOD</small> G<small>IRL</small> HEARS ABOUT THE TREE THE WAY all of them hear about it, after the terrible lords give their decree. The tree shocks them all, it frightens them really, and Blood Chief's daughter is no exception to this. Not in the hearing of it, anyway. But she is an exception in everything else, must always be an exception—so that, long before the story even begins, she is marked among all her kin of Xibalbá.

Oh, she has tightened her hair in defiant braids across the back of her head, of course, and has spoken too harshly once or twice to her father so that he is almost ready to do what they will both regret. But what daughter has not? Her eyes are like a jaguar's, and she has something that moves too lithely across her face. Her father might have always let the moments of paternal anger drift away. Perhaps because of her crisp rustle of skirts, with its hint of leaves. Even after it has gone, he can close his eyes and hear its faint shadow behind him. Or perhaps he feels that whatever discipline he takes will find its inevitable way back to be in her favor and then dissolve any hardness he might have affected. Because of his silence, the large cat beside her pupils licks its flanks everywhere in the house.

Blood Girl shoots up on her toes to look down the dark road toward Dusty Court, as if expecting the mysterious tree to suddenly appear over her father's shoulder, lumbering noisily down the road, its branches scratching the air, its fruit dangling and swollen. She peers slyly so that her father will not see what she is doing, but they both know. Her father's eyes suddenly darken, with some sadness, and fall across her brow in warning. She has been caught at this too much already, he feels, and says as much to the whole family. It is nothing but a girl's curiosity, her mother says in defense as she strokes his upper arm, his upper back, until he has been tamed.

And so, the story says, a maiden hears of the tree: the daughter of Blood Chief, Counselor Lord of Xibalbá, that barren town on a road north. And, when the news of the fruit-laden tree at Dusty Court reaches her ears, she is filled with wonder.

"One thing for sure," she says, "I must know what this tree is about. Surely, its fruit is really delicious. Pendulous."

Her parents say no for weeks. It is already a law disposed by the court. Your own father has signed on this. No! Unequivocably no, he says.

But she crouches for a moment at her night window, then leaps to quietly land on her feet. She goes by herself down the ball court road to catch a glimpse of the tree. She travels along the shadows, bounds across the clearings, to stand beside the tree. It is like a grave marker, gray and portentous. Hallelujahs given with upstretched arms, fingers spread wide. The bole, sleek. And the fruit is everything she has imagined.

She stands there a moment, unable to say anything, her fingers drawing aside her stray locks from her eyes. There is something delicious stirring within her belly. She feels herself undressed, except for the curious beads of longing that hang like opaline bracelets around her ankles, wrists, waist and neck. The spicy baubles rise, even, on the swells of her breasts.

Her teeth are set on edge against these beads.

"Oh," she says. "What fruit!" Her breath is cupped outside of her as she stares at the white fruit. "No, it would be wrong for you to be lost. Very wrong." She steps forward and the beads click softly against her flesh. "What if I should just cut one?"

Then a voice speaks harshly from among the leaves, "What do you want with just skulls made round on the branches of a tree?"

But this could be a handsome man's voice, concealed for now to find how strongly her eyes shine.

Her thin fingers cross her lips. She looks coyly down.

"You don't want them."

"Oh, I do," she says anxiously. "I do want them."

The silence is a single grape ripening purple on the vine.

"Then reach out, fair one. Reach your right hand out."

But her fingers tremble upon her lips.

"Don't you see?" the skull says. "Do you see me now?"

She nods and reaches right out, her right hand stretched out to the skull. White spittle falls in her hand. She feels its warmth, smells its pungent odor like bleach, then the spittle disappears, leaving only a viscous memory.

"This head of mine doesn't work," the skull says sadly.

Blood Girl gazes into the branches.

"It is just like the heads of great lords. There is the flesh, impressive at times, but the name is what is good. People take fright over bones, but there is no death in spittle; one's saliva is like one's essence. Whether the son of a lord or the son of a speaker, it is not lost but goes on; it remains whole. In sowing throughout the fallows, there is neither an extinguisher nor a destruction for the image of a lord or warrior, a sage or speaker. His daughters will remain, and his sons. Each carries the nourishment of the name further out into the world. There will always be a brightening for those who honor the living. So be it, as I have done to you."

And she feels the warm dampness of her hand voyage to the center of her heart. Her eyes purr in these cups.

"Climb up there to the earth. You shall not die. You shall enter into the world. Take to yourself the names of Former and Shaper, Majesty and Quetzal Serpent, K'ux Kah. Know them, and you shall join with what was begun at the start of the watch. Enter the concentric seas," says the skull of 1 Blowgunner, that white bone turned to fruit among the demon lords of hell.

And thus the maiden returns to her home, the seed dividing inside her: Blowgunner and Jaguar Sun. In four months, it is noticed by her father, Blood Chief.

He is beyond reason. Rather, he can see clearly what is right and wrong and the love he has for his daughter, but there is a man growing inside his flesh that can destroy whatever he may do. It is an angry man, not hateful, but filled with a blind emotion.

He has known for weeks that she is pregnant. He tries to remember whether he first saw it when she leaned once to pour water for his supper. She came forward so slowly and gently, the way a sapling turns tenderly forward in a breeze. And in the silent straining down, there is a struggle between opposing forces. Or was it as she sat across the dimly lit room, staring deeply into his eyes. The jaguar crouched tensely by her fathomless pools?

He says nothing harsh to her, forbids his females to speak of it, and the man inside is a monster. He beats his fist against the walls. These boomings are battle victories for her father. The women watch the struggle, have discovered how to help by fleeing quickly. But the creature howls every day, every day louder. All of them, even the stupid creature inside, know that it will win the war.

The howling comes at night; the axe splinters firewood with greater force; ropes are lashed together with the snap of whips; a clay urn shatters indoors. She tries to prepare for the hateful day. She twists her body in bed the way she knows she will later when the demon escapes. But the creature has no name, is forbidden to have a name. She has seen the battles and has winced. She has felt her cheek blister, her tears erupt, but without a name it is further than real. And once named, it *will* be real.

Then, when the man finally tears free, and sweeps his great paw into her face, it is a thunder she can almost cherish for having finally come from those horrible and uncertain depths.

"Damn you!" the monster screams at her. "Whore!"

She weeps from the ground, holding her face and tasting the blood of her mouth. She does not look at him, but waits in a heap for the creature to seek a more challenging foe. But this thing will roar equally as long as it was caged. Her mother no longer recognizes him, and says only what will turn his glare from her.

"My daughter is full of her fornicating!" he later roars at the other lords.

They gather to hear this sin: 1 Death, 7 Death; Flying Noose; Pus Maker, Bile Maker; Bone Scepter, Skull Scepter; Filth Maker, Wound Maker; Talon-Hawk, Snare, all the lords of Xibalbá.

"Question her about it," 1 Death says. "Ask her what this is."

"If she does not speak, she must be sacrificed," 7 Death says.

"Very well, my Lords."

"Who is father of your womb?" he asks her. His face is sweaty and his teeth grind behind his foul lips. He no longer cares for the mewling and purring of her eyes.

"I have no children," she cries. "Oh, Father, I have not known the face of any man."

There is a crack, worse than the first, that knocks her senseless at his feet.

"It is true that you are a fornicator! God damn you! God damn *you!*" He whirls on his feet, his face hating the sky.

"Take her!" he yells at the owls of Xibalbá. "Take her away from here. Bring her heart back to me so that the lords may examine it and we will know that the sacrifice was done!"

But when the four messengers carry away Blood Girl, the killing jar, and White Knife, the monster seems for a moment to have bellowed enough. Blood Chief peers out to see the servants of Death taking his daughter away.

"Perhaps," he whispers, "they will hear how gently beats her heart. See in her my once infant daughter." His words fall so airily that they pull apart, the way mists drift away above cold marsh reeds.

Even as they cross single file—these Owls and Blood Girl—the versant of a nearby hill, they recognize their peculiar kinship. They are all messengers, and will be messengers: carriers of things they never initiate, mouths of others, pliant vessels for the centered wills of others. They recognize this truth because of the light slanting blue-black that casts their silhouettes before them: Knife Owl, with his inflexible wings straight out like bristles; 1 Leg, with his unfortunate hopping and lame flapping; the featherless red skin of Parrot Owl creating a famished silhouette; and Skull Owl's incessant fluttering forming a halo around the others. And swollen among them, Blood Girl—cast out from her home.

Each of them understands their intimate connection as they walk silently, looking down at the commingling silhouettes that blend into new grotesqueries—the blades of Knife Owl extending out like quills from the goblet-shaped Blood Girl, while the rapid, fanning beat of Skull Owl's wings wheels round them both—or pull apart to once more reveal the ugliness of each of them. They recognize, one by one, that it is their bodies that have made them instruments for wills greater than they. Their bodies are shadows, silhouettes, of their essence.

The weight of this knowledge slows their step. As each discovers what is revealed before him, he follows more faithfully in single file. It is Skull Owl who understands it last. They cannot help but stop and look down at the final pattern formed by their alignment: a star with radiating points and a vibrant halo encircling it all.

"Oh look, my lords," Blood Girl says, tearfully. "It cannot be that you will kill me. We share. We have been united."

The truth is undeniable. They huddle as close as their peculiar bodies will allow.

"I was scorched and blistered," Parrot Owl says suddenly.

They want to hear this. It gives them something solid to trust, something more than their shadows cast before them.

"Our lords crippled me in a drunken anger," 1 Leg Owl says.

"Oh, messengers," she says, "my fornication does not exist."

They look into each other's face, seeing the sadness and the new relief brightening there.

"The life in my womb was just created. It was not my desire. I merely admired the head of 1 Blowgunner at Dusty Court. It was not my will."

"Nor mine," Skull Owl says angrily. "I did not ask to be held out to lions so that my anguish, my dismemberment, could serve as entertainment for others!"

The others see through Skull Owl's angry face. They understand the sweat of his brow, the tight, bunching muscles of his shoulders, the incessant straining in his face, the defiance in his eyes. They understand his humiliation. And something in their faces, looking up at him, releases the hard, dense ball lodged in his throat. He cries. He breaks under their compassionate eyes and allows his muscles to stop, his heart to unclench.

Skull Owl drifts tearfully to the ground, flutters a moment, then topples helplessly onto his face. His sobs rise from the dirt. The others dare not move. They cannot touch him for fear they will recall the dense ball, the clenched heart, and the tearless face.

Skull Owl lets his shame slowly expire amid the kindness of these others. He flips himself onto his back, and smiles to make words distant cousins to reality.

"Just coated with metal," Knife Owl confesses in turn. "They wanted me to be their sheriff, their cruel arm."

The others stand still. His strength is everywhere from him overpowering. He hangs his head in shame. "They ordered me to be master of Knife House!"

"Thank you," Skull Owl says to him from the ground.

Knife Owl looks down in confusion, then understands that Skull Owl has given him back his dignity, has accepted him just as they had accepted Skull Owl. He bends to help Skull Owl, but the other shakes his head, content to remain on the ground.

"We are not like them," Skull Owl says. "No matter what they do to us."

Knife Owl nods. He turns, nodding, to smile at Parrot Owl, 1 Leg Owl, and Blood Girl.

"Oh," he says suddenly, stepping back as if rocked by a blow. "What will we do? What can we put as a substitute for her heart? Think. We were told to bring her heart back so the lords may know their will was done. We must wrap it and drop the heart in the jar. Isn't that what we were told?"

"All right," she says, her eyes springing. "The heart doesn't have to be theirs, but then your homes will no longer be here. You have the power to force people to die, but you also have the power to fornicate, to beget. Then beget for 1 Death and 7 Death, only sap, only croton. Make my heart the blood of Cochineal. Beget this for them."

"We have lived dual lives already," the messengers proclaim.

"So be it," she says.

"So be it," they say.

Blood Girl smiles. "Then this heart won't be burned before them. Instead, take the fruit of that tree."

Red is the tree sap that she gathers in the jar, where it swells up round and sinewy. "It is called Cochineal Red Tree," she says, raising the blood of the croton above her head. The imitation hearts settles at the bottom of the jar.

Skull Owl flutters up from the ground and hovers there beside her. "This heart of yours will come back with us."

"Yes," she says, understanding his double meaning. "I will remain with you forever."

She reaches up to caress Skull Owl's face. "You will be loved on earth," she says. And to the others, reaching her hands out to one, then to the other, "There will come to be something of yours on earth. You will be loved."

"And you," Parrot Owl says coming forth, "shall carry up to earth our gift to you."

The Owls approach, one by one, and press their wings to her large belly.

"Our gift is full of wings," Parrot Owl says. "You will come to know this."

"Thank you, friends."

"Wait for us," Knife Owl says. "We must return with this false heart of yours."

So then they come before the lords, who are waiting expectantly. Parrot Owl holds out White Knife with the blood of the croton dripping from it.

"It is done, O Lords," Knife Owl says. "Here is her heart."

"Bring it here," 1 Death says, "that we may see it."

He pours it over a fire, the bark soggy with fluid, the bark bright crimson with sap.

"Stir the wood," he orders as the lords gather round.

And so, they burn the heart in the flames, these lords of death. And they stand like decrepit men, foul-tempered and ill, bent over the fire, their hands clasped behind their backs, and enjoying perversely the fragrance of a dying young heart.

Thus, as the lords crouch by the flames, the Owls return to guide Blood Girl past the dark road and up to earth. There, she touches their faces quickly, kindly—there is no time to speak even a single word—and hurries away. The Owls hurry away too, back to those lords who are still hunched forward with eyes ecstatically closed.

The messengers pause before the lords, then stand to one side, where they nourish thoughts of living things on earth; brighten with thoughts of how hell was defeated by a maiden—jaguar-eyed; deep, panther-eyed.

A MATTER OF TWINS

▼

Suddenly they were born, Blowgunner and Jaguar Sun, by name, but Xmucané did not watch it when Blood Girl found the day of their birth. She stayed by herself when the twins were born. She knew exactly when they appeared on the mountain and when they were taken into the house. She knew that 1 Monkey and 1 Howler did not sleep soundly with the arrival of their half-brothers. And it was not only because the twins did not sleep, but cried and made more noise so that Blood Girl forever catered to their needs.

"You should get rid of them," Grandmother said secretively. "They are loud-mouthed." It was an idea she planted in the fertile envy of the sons.

1 Monkey and 1 Howler snatched the twins from their beds and took them out to put in an ant bed, but they slept sweetly there. Then they placed them down on thorns, for that was what 1 Monkey and 1 Howler wanted: that the twins should die among the ants, carried away by flesh, or die bleeding on the thorns. They wanted it because of jealousy, red-faced anger. Yet these things did not work, so the brothers forced themselves, demanded their rights and would not allow the younger ones to live within the house.

The twins grew up in the mountains. They learned how to fashion blowguns and how to hunt for their food. They soon discovered that birds fell at their command. They did not need to shoot pellets, but they pointed their blowguns straight out and blew air. Theirs was a power over wings, their gift from the four owls. 1 Monkey and 1 Howler, however, were pipers and singers because they had grown up in great suffering. They had first learned the gentleness of the earth and then they had their mother die, their father and uncle die. In their loss, they learned to paint and to carve; their pain and torment made them great pipers, singers, painters and carvers. They understood the peace of the fields and not the violence of the woods. They wore loincloths and ankle bands, waist bells and colored fringes. They lay by the pools and watched the waters swirl. Everything was easy for them, the brothers thought. It was certain that they were now born. They were magicians and hunters, they came as substitutes for their fathers who had gone to Xibalá in honor of K'ux Kah, Former and Shaper.

1 Monkey and 1 Howler knew instantly everything in their own hearts when these younger brothers were born. But their sorcery didn't work against Blowgunner and Jaguar Sun, who spent all their time just hunting. It did not work in fact, because it was just hunting that the twins did all day. They had learned some things in the woods by themselves.

So when the twins brought to Grandmother the sharp talons of the hawk or the tusks of the peccary, 1 Monkey and 1 Howler shook the trees in anger. They would bring for their grandmother books full of the admirable deeds of heroes imagined for the glory of Heart of Heaven, huge silver platters with the earliest beginnings of the universe etched intricately throughout. Anxiously, 1 Monkey and 1 Howler took hold of their grandmother's sleeve, pulled her through the woods to see their intricate murals extending up the steep cliffs. They would point out for her the first flight of Quetzal Serpent, there among the natural rents in the rock, among the muscles of granite. They would say: see there, O Grandmother, see how we have painted you as that light which engenders all true life! There is Xpiacoc. There is the primordial sea. There is the search for language, for the words in the belly of Earth rising to her throat, and the struggle for nourishment. And there, O Mother, there is K'ux Kah enveloping us with love, enveloping everything, O Grandmother, sometimes as one, sometimes as three. And there: Look! Look! See how we are creators, too? And we are scribes for all that occurs."

She would smile at these two gentle sons, her eyes like a brimming sea.

But then, at her feet, Blowgunner and Jaguar Sun would come and place the extracted heart of some dark beast. They would drop back their heads and roar before Xmucané, their hands and arms covered with the blood of their struggle. They would find nothing of joy in the silver smithing, in the paintings, and nurtured, instead, a feeling of hungry worship for their grandmother.

And from this pairing of grandsons, of half-brothers, Xmucané would be in sorrow very much like the sorrow she discovered when her sons left for Xibalbá. "The world is so young," she explained to the older brothers. "My poor sons, the world is too young yet."

With time, 1 Monkey and 1 Howler found themselves looking more and more over their shoulders to see Grandmother sitting in her chair down the hall, the twins proud before her, and she looking into the eyes and hair of these new sons. The odor of their bloody hunts draped about them all like the mist of waterfalls. They tried to leave their carving of halls, their depiction of the feats of Former and Shaper, Blue Bowl Spirit and Green Plate Spirit. They tried to go into the woods and cut down the life of birds and animals. They were warriors, too, they wanted to say. They fought, you see, for their grandmother's love—these first artisans. But they could not bring back a limp body. Xmucané sat and watched them bring in catches, but they were small, harmless, and the brothers wept over their own carnivorous acts.

Instead, they shouted out, "We are done!" knowing that they were not finished with their new artistic creations, but they were only trying to steal some of the glory that Blowgunner and Jaguar Sun held tightly between their white teeth. They would turn awkwardly—fearing that their grandmother would turn away if they did not keep their eyes on her at every second—and they would point out what they had written, these artists, on unrolled bark.

"All my children!" she would say, and embrace Blood Girl, too, as if to obviate their unique configuration of pairs and halves and multiples of twos and special divisions by two. "It is fortunate, my children, that the world is coming along! It is fortunate."

But all this engendered a sadness in 1 Monkey and 1 Howler that they mistook for anger. They could not understand the greater glory of the twins.

"Why have you abandoned us?" they asked on a night when the sky was in a primordial whorl.

"Oh, no," she said. "I haven't. I really haven't. You will see, perhaps, what is planned for us all."

"Why do you love them more? Don't we brighten your existence? Don't we nourish the thought of you? Are we not strong with you? Don't we continue the name of our Lords?"

Xmucané pressed their faces against her breasts, as if to fill, somehow, the shame that now hollowed her heart. "Oh, no, no. It isn't that. No, my dear sons, I thank the womb of heaven that you have come to us. It's just my own doing. It's just my own failing." She cupped their faces to see into them. "It's just that the world is so young! We have tried to make a world that will only nourish, only brighten. We have learned the difficulty of this. Look, aren't your fathers dead? Haven't your fathers been defeated and haven't they left you to me as my sons? Aren't there, then, those who understand only the strength of arms? Aren't you afraid to do what the twins do with such pleasure?"

"Yes," they said, their faces enveloped softly within their grandmother's arms. She smelled like magnolias.

She kissed them each. "It's only because of this that your arts come too soon."

1 Monkey and 1 Howler accepted the hunting of the twins and continued their singing, their piping. Each had his office, they now understood. They painted and carved their respect for 1 Leg Lightning, Infant Lightning and Green Lightning, and turned away from the terrible bodies brought like bloody trophies to Grandmother. And they stifled the desire to point out, in retaliation, their own greatness crafted on walls, in books, in song, music, metals and cloth. They learned to cherish, instead, their grandmother's sad smile and whispered encouragement given them as she passed at night to her room. They learned to wait expectantly for her shadowed figure standing just within the light of their room, lingering for a moment like an apparition, and then smiling in such a way that it came as a sigh into the chambered hearts of the grandsons.

This is all that they learned to do in their solitary suffering. However, one night their grandmother did not stop, did not look down the hall to smile at her industrious grandsons chronicling the world on the marble walls and on the pages of *Popol Vuh*. Instead, she walked past them, her arms curled into the crooked arms of the twins. She passed without a nod, without a glance. From down the cold hallway, their grandmother's laughter seemed to the older brothers like a young girl's innocent surprise amid the harsh chattering of birds.

Because they were not loved by their grandmother, 1 Monkey and 1 Howler didn't give the twins food. Everything they reaped from the land was taken and eaten before they arrived. But the twins did not get angry or outraged by these actions. They endured it, as it is said, and knew their own essence. They knew the exact time of the world and that it was a time that encouraged them, not their half-brothers. Clear as light they saw this, so they accepted the stealing of corn and fruit so that nothing remained for them. They returned from hunting and discovered only a singing and piping left for them, rising unmolested from the woods and meadows.

Blowgunner and Jaguar Sun returned one day without anything. Grandmother looked to see them at the door, their arms glistening with the sweat of the hunt.

"Are there no birds?"

"We shot them, Grandmother, but they remained in the tree," they said. "There's no way of climbing after them, so we'd like our older brothers to go with us."

The grandmother called these other sons. She had Blowgunner and Jaguar Sun repeat to them what she was told.

"The time is near," she whispered to 1 Monkey and 1 Howler.

"All right, we'll go with you in the morning," they said.

Then the twins turned away, for the two of them had already finished their plan for 1 Monkey and 1 Howler.

The next morning, they went, these four, to the foot of Yax Tree. The air seemed to thunder and blacken with the number of birds within the branches. The twins immediately began to shoot, and the older sons were amazed when they saw the birds fall into the leaves. Not one fell to the ground. Some of the birds clutched the branches even in death, others fell to the crooks of the tree.

"Look," Blowgunner said. "Now you can see it, too."

"Yes," the sons said.

"We want you to help us by climbing up there. You do this better than we can do it."

1 Monkey and 1 Howler were pleased. They climbed up the tree, but the tree grew as they climbed and its trunk swelled rounder and rounder so that when 1 Monkey and 1 Howler wanted to climb down there was no way to descend. They called down feebly to their younger brothers, fearing the laughter they imagined would come because they could not even do climbing very well.

"We can't make it down," they shouted. "Help us!"

Blowgunner and Jaguar Sun struggled to see them above. The tree had grown so high that the two sons looked like small lights in the sky between the ceiba's branches. "Where are you?" they asked.

"It doesn't matter that you can't see us. Just help us get down!"

"Our voices sound so far away!"

"Never mind!"

Blowgunner and Jaguar smiled behind their hands. "Untie the sash of your loincloths and tie them under your bellies with a long end like the end of a tail behind you. If each of you uses this to drop down to each branch below you, then you'll be able to climb down."

The sons thought they would be able to lower each other through the precarious branches. Instantly, however, these sashes became real tails. And when the older brothers saw that they were now monkeys, they became frightened of their new faces and went fleeing along the trees of little hills and big mountains and finally found sanctuary in the forest. As they ran, the brothers screamed obscenities at the twins, but all that descended from the hoary canopy of trees was the simian hootings of monkeys.

Thus, with this revenge completed upon those older brothers who had done what they could to harass and bother them, the twins returned home to Grandmother. They allowed themselves to laugh as they went along home. They imitated the frightened look of their older brothers and clutched each other the way monkeys will do. They laughed even more than they should have because what they wanted was to arrive out of breath and colored, as if they had been running quickly to get their grandmother, when really they walked slowly.

"Something has happened to our brothers!" they said. "They went into the tree to find the birds, but everything transformed! The tree grew large and, suddenly, our brothers disappeared through the trees as though they were animals!"

Xmucané scolded them. "If you have harmed them, then you've made me unhappy. You will have done something wrong." Grandmother knew exactly what had happened, but she wanted the twins to learn some shame.

"Don't grieve, please. You'll see them again. It's only magic that made this occur, so piping and singing will bring them back. Come with us and watch, but this may be a trial for you, Grandmother. Don't laugh at all."

All of them returned to the edge of the forest, where the twins piped a song called "Blowgunner's Monkey," and sang the words, as well. They piped and danced as they had witnessed their brothers do before they had become monkeys, only the twins were not very good at this artistry, and they seemed to be just wriggling their bodies and jumping around in mockery of their brothers. Xmucané sat down at the foot of a tree.

Slowly, through the rustling of leaves, 1 Monkey and 1 Howler came dancing back, but when Grandmother saw their ugly faces and their dancing, she laughed just slightly and shamed them away.

"No," the twins said to her, "you can't laugh. Don't laugh. Don't even smile! Not even a tiny bit of teeth can show. Nothing."

The grandmother could not contain her laughter, especially to hear Blowgunner and Jaguar Sun plead for her not to laugh. It was as if everything was conspiring to make her laugh.

"What are you doing? We can only do this four times. So when you see their lips flapping don't laugh. Even when they return and stand like this with their faces sticking out and their hands scratching their butts. You cannot laugh. We can only do it three more times."

Even their pleading was humorous to Grandmother. Then they played again, waving their arms as they danced and making noises like monkeys through their lips. And they came again, these older brothers, only this time they came with erect penises bouncing to the rhythms of the music. "They seem ready for art now," the twins said. Grandmother sputtered with laughter.

"You've done it again," said Blowgunner and Jaguar Sun.

"All right," she said. "I promise. I won't laugh again."

But even as she spoke, she laughed so that Blowgunner and Jaguar Sun would not play anything until she stopped. Three times in all the brothers came and left. The twins piped and they came back. They were dancing, and the grandmother forcibly contained her laughter. Then they climbed up in the branches, their mouths pouting, their faces forlorn. And this time it was their bushy rears that sent Grandmother into peals of laughter.

"I promise I won't laugh," she said. "This time I know I won't laugh. I can do it."

And for the fourth time the music was played, but 1 Monkey and 1 Howler did not come back.

"We tried," 1 Blowgunner said. "We really did try. At first they came," he said, but again what the twins did was imitate the ridiculous manner of their brothers. "And then you laughed."

"Don't worry," she said. "They are my sons. They'll spread out into the world. They'll create and create throughout the years—and take some of my laughter, too! Really, they'll have their means and their ways."

"Our older brothers will be remembered," the twins said, and one put his hands under his arms, the other scratched his head.

"Seriously," she said. "They will be called upon by the pipers and singers, the formed people, also the painters and sculptors. Artisans will call them. They will bring joy to everyone. They will pester conquerors later on, in their red clothes."

The old text says that they became monkeys because they boasted and mistreated their younger brothers according to the manifestation of their hearts. But it was what Former and Shaper saw ahead, and it was also the humble nature of artistry to blame the self. It was through suffering that 1 Monkey and 1 Howler became artists. It was in their gentleness that they became pipers and singers, painters and sculptors. And during the time that Former and Shaper were setting right their mis-beginning, these creators were better let loose in the world that was as yet pairing and dis-pairing infinitely outward. And in their artistic creations, to beget a nourishing view that would beget more and live longer through a language more profound than force.

THE UNHAPPY LIFE OF
THE FALSE SUN AND MOON

▼

I<small>T WASN'T UNTIL THE TENTH DAY OF HIS</small> marriage that 7 Parrot discovered virtue in extracting metals from the earth. It began in the simplest of ways, but the curious mind of 7 Parrot soon found new and complex ways of extraction.

After working in the cornfield one day, 7 Parrot went to the river to drink. Bending down, he noticed yellow flecks shifting in the sand below. He tried, rather naively, to pinch out the gold with his fingers. He failed and attributed the failure to the partition of water. Instead, he scooped out a handful of sand and placed it into his cupped shirt. The water drained away, leaving a pile of gold-streaked sand. He again tried to pick away the minute flecks, but it was really a hopeless task.

The flecks that he managed to pull out were not enough to cover a fingernail. Still, he was anxious to show his find to his wife, so 7 Parrot decided to save the gold by putting it between his gums and front teeth. It was painless and efficacious.

Later, in a playful mood, 7 Parrot merely smiled to show off the gold. Shield Bearer was duly impressed. She took her husband's arm, scratched a fingernail up to his elbow, and pulled him close to her breasts.

"My Lord!" she said with teeth set on edge.

7 Parrot kissed his wife, then tried to pull a step back to be marveled at again. Shield Bearer had other plans, however, and had marveled enough in

this passive way.

She stepped tightly against her husband and slowly undid the clothes that bound him. A deep heat matured within 7 Parrot as she ran her fingernail across his nipples, along the muscles of his belly so that they twitched beneath the skin. She kissed his hip bone, softly, suckingly, her admiration full of tongue.

7 Parrot smiled brightly, which only stoked Shield Bearer's desire.

She stroked her husband's brightly colored beak with her hand and whispered, "Macaw. Lord. Sweetie-Pie!" She rubbed the red and yellow feathers of his cheek back toward his neck, making him flinch with passion. "I love you," she said, and removed his trousers from around his scrawny ankles.

7 Parrot smiled abundantly and nodded his head, his long beak rising and falling to the sensuous rhythms she set up in him. His breath was unable to gather voice, unable to gather words that would nourish them.

Even so, their lovemaking reached a tenderness and passion which filled them with wonder. Wrapped in each other's arms, they could not comprehend anything of the world outside their love. Thus, it was with difficulty that 7 Parrot freed himself from his wife's arms the next morning to go and work in the cornfield. They argued viciously with their touches and tongues both of them arguing against working that day—but shadowing those same arguments was the argument that won: that their reunion would be even more ardent.

7 Parrot worked the corn that morning with a preoccupation that fired him at times to work feverishly—perhaps to finish quickly and return to the arms of his wife, which now seemed an immense cocoon of love, or perhaps merely to obliterate the image of her languorous stare that urged him to forsake his work. As it was, he would work for a time, then stare into the air and allow his desire for Shield Bearer to consume him, to build in him a series of images that built upon each other with such speed that their connections seemed mystical, magical, beyond any shaping or forming, beyond any guiding frame.

Once, as he stared thus, he noticed egg dripping from the bottom of a nest. He climbed the short distance to look more closely and found two whole eggs and the scattered shell of a third. He recalled the fluid as it had first protruded from the nest like a translucent twig, became globular, then dropped under its own weight.

This image brought back, first, the image of their passionate lovemaking, then the image of his gold-flecked teeth reflecting in Shield Bearer's dark eyes. He saw, then, the lump of sand by the river with its tiny gold flecks.

Instantly, 7 Parrot envisioned the viscous and loving gaze of his wife pouring through the nest. It was here that he suddenly realized the knowledge emerging from that infinite sea of images. He pulled the nest from the tree and joyfully kissed the two speckled eggs. Then he ran to the river, where he scooped sand into the nest, but the sand, mud, and gold flecks drained thickly through the loose-fitting twigs. All that remained were stones—though some quite pretty. Soon, however, he managed to pan a nugget of gold. It was the size of his littlest tooth.

At that very moment, he resolved to lead his life in the pursuit of gold, on the netting of the river; and he snapped a maturing stalk of corn growing beside the insidious river.

▼

Ah. The lovers' passionate cries sprang from their throats as birds do, sharply, from vermilion hills, and the air burst with their vespertine fervor as the sky shocks in storm.

▼

"It is from that moment on," 7 Parrot recounted to Shield Bearer as they lay in bed, "that I gave up farming. There is nothing but the ordinary in it. I see, truly, the pathetic lives of our wooden cousins. I see how meek, how homely and unimaginative those splinterable lives are. I have come home with gold in my teeth! I have stood before my wife with the sun a parturition of my mouth. You have turned my life from one of drabness to one of passion." He touched his wife's smiling face. "It is really you who have sloughed off the dross."

"I love you," she said.

7 Parrot kissed the curve of her shoulder. "You are Happiness. You've taught me the purpose of my life, how to bring joy to our hearts. I love you. Oh, I love you. And together, there's nothing we can't feel, nothing of passion we will not have as our own."

Shield Bearer blushed with his excitement. "Then it's good," she said, "that you give up farming."

He crashed into her arms, so entangling them that they possessed at once the violence and the beauty of a newborn fledgling which tears into life through the roundness of shell.

"As for me," Shield Bearer said finally, solemnly, nearly breathless by their intimate struggle; she placed the flat of her hand over his breast, "I've decided to shadow you. Where you thrive, so will I. Where you breathe, my happiness abounds."

7 Parrot stroked her moon face. "Our love is enough."

"I'm your shadow," she said. "I choose it."

▼

The next day, 7 Parrot went to the river to pan for gold. He took with him the bird nest, a large cloth, a pot and a bag, and prepared to experiment for hours. He first sifted through the mud and sand by using the bird's nest, but felt it wasteful to let the gold flecks drain away. Instead of letting a particularly glittery pile of sand go by the way of the nest, he put it into his pot and resolved to go through it later, fleck by fleck. 7 Parrot managed to find several pieces of gold large enough to be captured by the nest, but the waste of gold flecks nagged at his growing desire to have every minuscule piece.

So, by the time he finished playing with the nest and had thought to look at the sand he had left in the pot, the pile had dried in the air. He looked dumbly into the pot, not having a clue as to how to begin the extraction, and *harumphed* through his nose. The air spread over the sand and whisked away the minute grains. He noticed, though, that the flecks of gold tended not to move as easily as the sand. He *harumphed* again and again into the pot to check if what he had noticed was correct or not. It seemed to be. He also discovered that the breath from his nose was better than the breath from his mouth. So he sat for hours, blowing the soft grains of sand to the side of the pot, and in this way—*humphing* and *harumphing*—7 Parrot cleared enough sand away so that he could dip his fingers into the pile and pinch away gold.

But he grew impatient with this—and not a little hyperventilated. He conceived of drying the lumps of sand over a wood fire. He placed another pile into the pot. In this manner, he managed not only to indelibly blacken the bottom of the pot, but managed as well to dry out the sand at a faster rate than time alone could have done. With this new batch, 7 Parrot proudly squatted and airbrushed the sand with his long nose.

All in all, for the first day out, 7 Parrot amassed a respectable cache of gold. The trouble was that he wanted the gold to be in a unified form—say, tiny sheets to place over his teeth—not flecks and nuggets or gold-speckled stones. The desire alone set off a course of events that ended in its effect. Because, as the old book says, ideas are things, hard as stone.

7 Parrot recalled how the many volcanoes made a pudding of rocks, trees, and not just a few animals. From that moment on, he was committed to the development of heat as the unifying system. Then there was only for him to devise the correct stacking of stones and earth to funnel heat in the most controllable fashion. Once he had made his furnace, he soon discovered the various melting points of different materials. It wasn't long before he created a metal pot and attempted his first smelting of gold.

His early attempts taught him the problem of separating gold from iron, gold from bronze, gold from limestone. He wasted his precious gold as quickly as he extracted it, with nothing more to show for it but curiously plated pots and pans and long handled thongs.

It wasn't until he had invented enough utensils to equip any home, that he discovered he needed very little heat to smith his flecks and tiny gold nuggets into fine gold sheets. It was just as well, for the various things he had created during his Stone Age, Iron Age, and Bronze Age, were then used to refine and decorate the gold he now panned with ease. And after weeks and months, 7 Parrot and Shield Bearer stepped from their home and into the dull wine light of the world. They shone as bright as their love.

There was no sun or moon at this time, only the brightening from these two who glorified themselves. Only their vainglory lit up the sky, as everywhere the first people disseminated and diversified so that among their multiplicity there would be one who said the names of the true Sun and Moon.

Dressed in quetzal feathers, leg trappings, ear pins, nose plugs and gold threaded clothes, 7 Parrot exclaimed: "I am great and shall rule over the first people. I am the sun and light; you are the moon and shadow. Great is our brightness. We are the track and the path for the world. Our eyes are silver, our faces green jade, blue turquoise. When we walk through the day, the people will say that the sun has arisen. They will say that the moon is close behind. They will cry out that to live in the shadow of the sun and moon is to find boundless joy."

Shield Bearer looked at her husband and smiled roundly with her gold covered teeth. Gold dots hung beneath her eyes, in her ears were long pieces of green jade, interlaced with gold. Her fingernails were rounded in jewels.

"We are the creators, we, parure of the earth," 7 Parrot said as he looked at his beautiful wife. He stroked her face. "The pith and joy of my existence is your face."

Shield Bearer touched her husband's golden arm. She ran two fingers from his beak, down his feathered chest, to the warmth bulging behind a golden brooch. "Make love to me," she said.

▼

Such was their ardor that the couple soon produced two sons: Cayman and 2 Leg, by name.

"Behold me, I am the sun!" 7 Parrot said.

"Behold me, the moon," Shield Bearer said.

"Behold Maker of Earth!" said Cayman, the older son.

"And it is I who shake the universe and crack the earth," said 2 Leg.

Just as the parents had done, so the sons took their greatness as a matter of fact. It was this that Heart of Heaven saw clearest. Thus, the Blowgunner twins were made to destroy the mighty family of earth movers and earth makers, sun and moon. The twins, Blowgunner and Jaguar Sun, heard the boasting done by the family, and they recognized it as evil. Jaguar Sun and Blowgunner were children of gods, so they understood that it was not good that the family did not respect Heart of Heaven and not good that the four did not even know a single one of the million names of god.

"People won't be able to live around here," Blowgunner said about 7 Parrot. "It will be a disaster if he keeps to his bragging because all people might become like him. Let's try to shoot him after he eats. We'll make him sick and then take away his wealth. We'll take away his jewels, his silver and jade, his treasures that make him too proud."

"Such glory is mere metal," Jaguar Sun said, speaking of the Parrot family.

"One son goes about creating volcanoes just to show off," Blowgunner said.

"That is Cayman."

"The other moves around the earth, shaking his body and destroying the mountains."

"2 Leg, who brags by destroying," Jaguar Sun said. "He thinks that destroying proves strength, and refuses to nourish our First Mother, our First Father."

"Doesn't he know that destroying is the easiest thing?"

"He doesn't know it," Jaguar Sun said. "He doesn't see the inevitability, the weakness."

In this way, the twins planned the shooting of 7 Parrot as he fed from his nance tree. The false sun climbed the branches every day to pick the fruit that grew ripely from the tree. The twins understood this fact. Sometimes, he would sit for hours, lazily sucking the pulp, enjoying the rolling of juice along his tongue, the nourishment filling his mouth and belly, before returning home with the choicest fruits for his wife. All this, the two sons knew.

Jaguar Sun and Blowgunner decided to linger by the nance and shoot him with their blowguns as he descended from his palatal indulgence. It was really no difficult thing for them to hide among the bushes, rise up when 7 Parrot climbed down, and shoot their blowguns. They did it easily. 1 Blowgunner aimed his pellet and fired into the serrated jaw of 7 Parrot. The blow sent him sprawling to the ground, heaped in confusion. Blowgunner ran to grab him, but by the end of the tussle it was the arm of 1 Blowgunner which was grabbed. 7 Parrot reached forward a bit, then down so that the arm cracked away from the shoulder with the sound of a relenting hull. He did not beat the sons, did not make an end of their molestation, but simply took Blowgunner's arm home with him, cursing as he went.

"Those two tube-suckers broke my jaw!" he said to Shield Bearer. He placed the arm on the wall above the fire. "Even my teeth hurt! And my eyes. What did I do to them?"

Shield Bearer helped her husband to bed and gently coaxed him to lie flat. The glint of gold from his mouth made her hand tremble above his waist. She brought him a paste of tobacco and mint, and rubbed her finger along his gums until she felt faint with wetness.

"Why is there evil in the world?" 7 Parrot asked. "It doesn't make sense."

"Be careful of jealous people," his wife said. She lay beside him, her cheek against his iridescent chest.

Elsewhere, Jaguar Sun and Blowgunner discussed ways to get back the arm and to end the life of the false Sun and Moon. They turned to Xmucané and Xpiacoc for advice. The two old Gods were all white like sun bleached shells. Humbled and bent over like hunchbacks, they were also called Grandmother and Grandfather.

"We'll go to the house of 7 Parrot," Blowgunner said, "and pretend that we're your grandchildren."

Jaguar Sun continued, "Say to them that our mother and father are dead and that we follow you everywhere. Tell them that you are interested in getting rid of us because all you do is remove jawbugs and there is no good living in this."

" 'There's no money to be had in removing jawbugs'," Blowgunner quoted for them to say.

"Very well," Grandmother and Grandfather said.

The four of them dressed in old rags and smudged clothing, and they walked before the house of 7 Parrot and Shield Bearer.

7 Parrot, on his throne at the doorway, groaned. "Where are you going, Grandfathers?" he asked.

"Just looking after ourselves."

"Aren't those your children with you? You seem to be on a journey. Aren't they looking after you?"

"Not at all, Lord," they said. "They're our grandchildren, our descendants. We feel sorry for them, instead of them watching out for us. We give them a share of what we have, a portion of what is ours, Lord."

The mouth of 7 Parrot gaped widely as he moaned with pain. "I wish that you'd feel sorry for me."

"What happened?"

"Injustice! Evil in the world! I am the Sun, just wanting a nourisher and instead there is torment. I tell you, one must be careful. Can you cure anything?"

"We only remove jawbugs and cure eyes," they said. "We can set bones, too."

"Perfect," 7 Parrot said. "I can't sleep from the pain that those two devils caused me. They shot me in the eye and jaw. I haven't been able to eat because of it. I'll surely die if nothing is done."

The grandfathers approached the throne and peered into his mouth. "Those two must have shot some kind of magic into you. It seems there's some kind of bug eating your jaw. It must have flown on secret wings to do this bitter thing. The only way is to remove your teeth."

7 Parrot shook his head. "Oh, no," he said. "That isn't a particularly good idea." He looked into the house to see if Shield Bearer was listening, and felt a curious tightening in his groin. "It would be a very big loss. You have no idea."

"It's the only way."

"You don't know what's at stake. These teeth of mine do more than eat food."

"Don't worry," the grandfathers said. "We'll replace them with teeth made of ground bone so that you'll look as radiant as before." Then to help 7 Parrot decide, Grandfather pushed the jaw just enough to make the pain shoot up into 7 Parrot's skull.

"All right," he said. "All right. Take out my teeth, but give me new ones. And don't let my wife know about this."

And instead of teeth made of ground bone, the grandfathers put in white corn. These false teeth gleamed for an instant from the white dough, then at once 7 Parrot's face fell like an old man's. With the blue and gold inlays out, he no longer looked like a lord. And when the eyes were fixed on 7 Parrot, he no longer had the silver and gold dots. Instead, he looked like an ancient bird, tawdry and mite-ridden. The pride fell from him like wet earth.

In this way, the brightness of 7 Parrot flickered away, and broke even the heart of his moon shadow. All that was left was the paleness of flesh.

Cayman and 2 Leg buried their parents after four days of mourning. To emulate their once fiery splendor, the two sons built a pyre of dogwood and *ocote*—that turpentine heart of pine. Once lit, the flames scorched the air in rabid colors. First brilliant orange, then yellow—a yellow that filled the sky—then red and the colors of sunset. And what was left was the blue ash of the moon.

MAKER OF MOUNTAINS

ONCE THE EARTH CASCADED OVER THE URN OF their parents, the two sons walked away from each other as silently as they had been throughout the funeral. What had bound them together was the grandeur of their parents. It had restrained their opposite natures, their exclusive greatness. For as sons of the Sun and Moon, they were also Maker of Mountains and Destroyer of Mountains. What Cayman did during the day, 2 Leg destroyed behind him; what 2 Leg destroyed and rubbed flat against the surrounding earth, Cayman found as potential mountain. With their parents alive, they had been complementary under the brilliance of their great light. Urned and interred, the light of their parents now only illumined for each his singular purpose.

They walked silently apart, these two brothers.

They both stopped once to look across the way, but only a nod, only a movement of the head was what occurred between them. Lolling his huge head to one side was Cayman, and then farther away, on the other side of the world, there was 2 Leg with his massive teeth, lumbering away.

This is what happened after the death of 7 Parrot and Shield Bearer, the false sun and moon.

Cayman walked westward until he found a great expanse of land which was as flat as Green Plate Spirit, not far from the lands of some formed people, some shaped people. This was before the rain of glue, the resin-filled sky. He climbed up to a craggy precipice of a newly formed mountain to hurl himself like a stone from the ledge. He envisioned a long descent, the valley filling to the brim with his loud shriek of sorrow as he plummeted to death. He would cry out his mother's name, then his father's in a long and soulful complaint. But as he stood high above, he looked down upon the village of wooden people and saw their huts, star-strewn with house fires. He saw their dark shadows moving as if by gusts of wind from one hut to the next. They seemed like mindless thistles, subject to whatever currents ruled their direction, sent them wafting this way and that in fatuous progressions. From that height, he understood more perfectly the greatness of his parents. They had been the true sun and moon. They had found the way to make something of the earth, to be more than mere puppets. They were creators. This was his legacy, as well. As the son of 7 Parrot and Shield Bearer, his destruction would be to admit something wrong.

"I am Maker of Mountains," he said aloud, his fist tight against his chest.

He set himself the devotion to create a mountain which, by its magnificence alone, would be a testament to his parents' divinity. His parents would tower above everything else in the world, and he, as builder, would be the sun's foundation, the moon's base, the solid earth to their heavenliness.

By day, he undertook his embracive search of the land; by night, he stood atop his work and challenged the false gods who rumored the land like jackdaws. To the north, he went to collect the gypsum white stone, then the next day to the south where sulfurous earth lay. Thus, he brought red, sapphire earth from the east and from the west—stupidly, perhaps—a peat rich soil which denied like the future all the certain hues of directions. He formed in his mind the beauty of the trees and the flourishing of plants; he shaped in his thoughts the brightening of the mountain, so that it became inevitable that he would succeed. The sky became clearer, roseate, as his thoughts became manifest. The air crackled and the ground moaned as in the deep swells of love. The mountain jutted up into air from the rent and pungent earth.

He finished the mountain, called Meavan, and covered his eyes with his hands. He allowed mourning to enshroud him. "I am Maker of Mountains," he whispered.

How different he was from the 400 sons who lived nearby. The 400 sons of the formed people who were to fall beneath the maws of pots and the scissoring of plates. Each had come to know the name of K'ux Kah. Each had fought to correct the evilly ignorant ways of his parents and neighbors, and each had upset, zealously, the wooden peace of his village. Then, as zealots, they congregated in private. They exacted a kind of cruel devotion from each other, and believed to their bones the harsh judgment of K'ux Kah.

In their manner, however, it was not K'ux Kah to whom they prayed, but to the panthers of night which took the names of Blowgunner Bird, Serpent Hawk and Former, Shaker. Daily, they put upon stone altars the smoke-drugged bodies of devotees to carve out their beating hearts. In the name of Dios, they cudgeled a sacrifice to death, then burned his heart and eyes in small pyres of wax and pine. Their screams of adoration ripped through the air like the terror screaming through their twisted image of heaven. Theirs was a warrior holiness, which made a convert or a sacrifice out of anyone who happened upon their sacred land. Because of this, their ardor was an oasis: the encircling sands were blood red and their island a miasma.

II

Cayman, feeding at the base of a grand waterfall, saw the 400 sons pass down from his mountain. They had cut a giant cross-beam from his forest and struggled under the immense weight.

Cayman called out. "What are you doing?"

"Carrying a tree," they said.

Cayman approached.

"Don't worry, we can lift it," they said.

"Shoulder it a bit higher and I'll help you. I'm strong. By the by, this is a very fine tree. A beautiful tree. A magnificent tree."

"The woods here are truly a marvel," the 400 said. "The mountain just appeared, just came into being—thank the Lord—and it is filled with strong trees, birds, and deer. The waters from it never cease. They are brimming with life. We fish with baskets held out above the rivers."

Cayman was pleased with their love of Meavan. "Have you heard of Sun and Moon?"

"We are waiting for the sun," they answered. "It hasn't appeared. When it comes, all of the chosen ones will leave this unfortunate earth and sit in the lap of God, the womb of heaven, Tears, as it is called by us, the faithful."

Cayman lifted the huge tree and carried the greater part of it over his own shoulder. "Do you know the names, 7 Parrot and Shield Bearer?"

The 400 sons just huddled at the back. "Neither," they answered. They saw the great brow of Cayman, his expansive back, his muscles bulging and persistent.

"What are you building?" he asked.

"It's the crossbeam of our Great House. It is to honor God. When the sun comes, God will come. This is what we mean by waiting for the dawn. Do you worship, my son?"

Cayman lifted the beam more securely. Silently, broodingly, he carried the tree to their door.

The 400 sons did not ask again. They merely walked and followed Cayman's broad back. But at their home they said, "Stay with us and eat."

"Truthfully, I should go."

"Where are your mother and father?"

"I am Maker of Mountains," he said. When the others only smiled politely, he answered, "I have no parents."

"Then stay. You have helped us and we must return the favor. We are all children beneath Serpent Hawk."

Cayman nodded. "Children of Gods," he said ambiguously.

"We can pay you. Every day we need wood chopped. We need more beams and posts. We seek the glory of Grandmother and Grandfather. You can earn your way here."

"Fine," Cayman said.

But after eating, after speaking and discovering just enough about each other—Cayman and the 400 sons—after nourishing themselves and brightening their spirits, the 400 sons took counsel apart from Cayman.

"Did you see him?" they said to one another. "What are we going to do with him?" They shook their heads, remembering Cayman's gnarled muscles, the pillars of his legs, the magnificent cords of his neck.

Cayman slipped quietly by to listen.

"It's not good what he does," they said. "He lifts a beam all by himself."

"He says nothing of God."

"Who knows what harm he can do us?"

"Let's dig a big hole—" some said.

"No!" others answered. "Make *him* dig a hole!"

"Have him dig it and then make him go down. 'Just lift the dirt out for our beam,' we'll say to him. When he's bending over, we'll throw it on top of him."

"Killing him is truly the best thing."

The next day, they dug a shallow hole and called out to Cayman. "We can't do this," they said. "Help us by going down. Dig until we say that the hole is deep enough. Call up when the dirt is dug out so that the hole is truly deep."

"Yes," he said and began to dig. Only the hole he dug was to prove his parents, by making a mirror image of the mountains he made. The 400 sons knew nothing of him. They knew nothing of 7 Parrot and Shield Bearer. They knew nothing of the true sun and moon. They were waiting for God when the Gods had already come and gone. He was here, yet they knew nothing of him. Therefore, he dug a branch, a cavern, into one side of this inverse mountain.

"How far are you?" they asked as dirt spit up from the hole.

"I'm digging," Cayman said. "You must wait." He worked like an alligator, heaping up a mound to lay the rubbery eggs of his deception.

The sons whispered among themselves. "There is so much dirt that if the beam doesn't kill him, he will surely suffocate."

Once safe within the branch of the hole, Cayman called to them. "Come on now. Take the dirt out. Maybe you can't hear me. I've dug very deep. Hello?"

The boys smiled and shouted down, learning the dental pleasure hidden within their own plan.

"There's your call," Cayman said. "Only it seems as if it's very far away, doubly far away, perhaps. Down here, it echoes deeply. It echoes like death from here."

As Cayman spoke, he heard the boys dragging their large beam to the edge. Then he smelled the rain of dirt as the weight of the tree crumbled the hole's mouth. And the instant the beam dropped into view, Cayman screamed; he let loose a groan which echoed out with the thud of the beam.

"He's finished!" they said. "He's dead! This is all there is of him."

Each of the 400 felt a certain strength lodged firmly in his will.

"Just think what would have happened if he had kept on doing what he was doing!" they said to each other. "He would have imposed himself among us!"

"Among us: the devoted 400 sons!"

"No one can imagine this."

They looked at one another with greater appreciation of their deed. "How would it be with someone like him ruling over us?" they asked.

Not one could answer such a question, as divine purpose was inscrutable. But in their victory, confident and selfish, a very distinct and different K'ux Kah was assumed.

"See what their God is," Cayman thought.

"When we come back the day after tomorrow," the sons said, "and we see the ants coming from the hole with the flesh of that monster, then our hearts will be set right. We will feel safe. Then we will drink our sacred wine."

Cayman, sitting in the hole, heard what the boys discussed about the day after tomorrow, so that on the second day, when the ants assembled, they did run out, streaming, with Cayman's flesh. Then the boys saw the ants come out with the hair of Cayman. The ants fled from the hole like a decadent thread of flesh.

"Look," the boys said, "see the fingernails of that creature? The ants are bringing out the body bit by bit. Even if they assemble him," they said, "he will be nothing but a patchwork. He won't have his strength except in parts." The 400 sons laughed at their joke.

But down in the hole, it was Cayman's laughter which was growing. It was his hair which the ants carried from the hole, but it was the hair that Cayman had pulled from his living head. The ants carried the fingernails which Cayman had chewed from his own fingers, not what the ants themselves had pulled from rotting flesh. The 400 sons laughed, but Cayman smiled with a white laughter blossoming in his belly.

With their victory, the 400 sons began to drink. They went home and brought out their wine. They rolled up their cigarettes and smoked until the smoke curled from their foreheads. They drank and smoked until they knew nothing more than the insalubrious visions inside their heads, burbling through their sidetracked veins: a sight of God too terrible, too simple in their devotions.

Cayman crept through the village at nightfall. He lifted his great tail so that it would not brush against walls and arouse the sons. He slipped carefully to the sacred house and listened by the door. Just drunken snoring and farting was what he heard. Cayman slid a talon between his teeth as if tasting again an opulent meal.

"I work in the name of 7 Parrot," he said. "In the name of Shield Bearer." Then he pushed against the wall with all his might until the timber groaned and the center beam cracked. Suddenly, the sacred roof collapsed upon the drunken 400, so that all that was left of them was the marc of their decadence.

"This is the truth of your wine," Cayman said.

Not even one or two were left.

"Now we shall truly honor Sun and Moon," Cayman decreed.

He hunted the mountains and the valleys for crabs and fish, deer and peccary. "All things shall be of nourishment to Thee," he said, his arms upstretched to the sky, his heart rapid with adoration of his parents. "All things shall brighten You."

Upon his mountain altar, Cayman glorified 7 Parrot and Shield Bearer with a gigantic meal which ended all creatures within twenty leaps. There he decimated his catch. One tenth for himself, the rest for the greater glory of Parrot Stock. He gorged himself on this mountain of game until he fell asleep. Carrion birds spiraling down to feed on the offerings only became what they themselves had sought when Maker of Mountains suddenly rose up from sleep. In this devotion, Cayman made sure that everything in his vicinity knew the proper Gods, since he was soon the only thing which survived.

III

Just following the word of Heart of Heaven were Jaguar Sun and Blowgunner. They knew that Cayman went about fishing and crabbing during the morning and afternoon, and carried mountains by night. They planned the creation of a huge crab. They put crowsfoot for its face—the kind picked from out in the bush—and bamboo for its claws. They also put shells for its legs and cut stone for the resounding crab's back. Then they put this shell at the bottom of a cave at the very bottom of the great mountain called Meaven.

The sons walked along to find Cayman in the water and asked him where he was going.

"I am not going anywhere," Cayman said. "I'm hunting."

"What kind of food?"

"Fish and crabs, but there are no more. Two days ago, I ate the last." Cayman looked a little hungrily at the arms and legs of the twins. "Do you know Sun and Moon?"

Jaguar Sun and Blowgunner did not answer that. "You must be looking in the wrong places," they said instead, "because there's a crab down there in the canyon. A really huge crab. If you're lucky, you can probably eat him. He just bit us. We tried to catch him, but we got frightened. Unless he's gone, of course, you would be able to catch him."

"Have pity on me," Cayman said. "Show me where it is."

"We don't really want to. You go. It isn't hard to find. We'll explain the way. Just go along the river—that way—until you come to Meavan. Follow downstream, of course, until you come to the etched hill. Follow the water into the cave. You'll discover it at the foot of the mountain. It's rustling there at the bottom of the canyon. The crab is so large, so proud, that it would be very difficult not to see it."

"Nonetheless, have pity on me," Cayman said. "He won't be found. Come along and I'll show you birds along the way. You can shoot them. I know where they all are, those which are left."

"Well," Blowgunner said, "actually, you might not get him. He was moving when we saw him. We managed to trick him toward us, but then we were bitten. He's very strong. We went down, and at first he was frightened because we were crouching as we went down. He must have thought we were more powerful, but we couldn't get him. It might be good for you to crouch when you go down."

"I don't understand what you're talking about."

"Which word didn't you understand?" the twins asked.

"I understand each word quite well, I believe. It's more a matter of their arrangement, perhaps."

The twins knew this statement about words was quite true. "Well, we'll show you, then. You'll understand without our words to guide you."

"Thank you," Cayman said.

They traveled together to the bottom of the canyon where, to one side, the crab lay still. Bright red was his shell, at the bottom of the canyon.

"Excellent," Cayman said. He wished that it would just go into his mouth, because he was starving.

Cayman tried to go down flat, but wouldn't fit. He tried to go in crouching, but the crab stayed beyond reach. Cayman came back out.

"Didn't you get it?" the twins asked.

He looked at his hands, at the faces of the twins. "Isn't it obvious that I didn't? He's just crouching there between the rocks."

"It would probably be good if you went in upside down," the boys said. "A change of position, you know, a new partition."

It was true that he could not get the crab the way he had tried. He could not think of anything else to try. "All right," Cayman said and crouched upside down with only his kneecaps showing.

The twins waited until Cayman slipped into the sheets of the cavern, into the crevasses of the mountain he had created, then they severed the granite tendons. With a monstrous groan and spasm, Meavan crashed down on Cayman like a fat lover. And there, as the dust lifted off, as the colossal weight slowly nuzzled, a final vision of his mother came squeezing out of Cayman's head.

Blowgunner and Jaguar Sun whisked the scattering of dust from their sandals.

THE NORTH IS WHITE

▼

"I AM DESTROYER OF MOUNTAINS," HE
SAYS, but it is really Blowgunner and Jaguar Sun who destroy *him*.

2 Leg moves northward where the earth turns against the sky like white
waves at storm. It is this exact color which he seeks. Not wittingly, but when
he comes upon the bleached ground, he stops and smiles with his gigantic
teeth. In the whiteness of the north, he sees the perfect melding of all colors,
the swirling to nothing of that which might have had distinctions. He smiles and
feels a kind of happiness crawl over his flesh. This white joy surprises him
because it has seemed lost forever since the death of his parents. And for him,
this is his decision to stay.

He has moved across the land, stamping his feet and tearing down the
hilltops. He has screamed like a *tepesquintle*, has wept for his parents' death.
Unlike his older brother, who turns sadness into a monument, 2 Leg distills his
into a black pool of bile.

He first stays around the wet decadence of swamps. He takes perverse
pleasure in the way the earth sucks at his feet as if pulling him into the entropic
glue. The downward pulling, the black assimilating of the swamps seems, to
him, to mirror his heart. The fact that his parents were murdered only deepens
the tar inside him.

So he stays for a time, stamping and roaring at the sky, weeping at night in
the dark envelope of his sadness. In the day, he walks slowly from his swamp
and investigates the hills that spread ever outward. At the edge of the morass,

which also spreads gradually out, 2 Leg bends over to scrape the dry earth into the wet sucking earth. Crouching down with gray rags and tattered clothes, he seems an ancient stone thrust upon the ground. His hair has long ago grown thick with the moss of this home and seems Medusan in its dark green entanglement. Even the odor of his body is indistinguishable from the morass surrounding him.

In this way, 2 Leg walks to the hills to wreak destruction upon their skyward leaning, lowing as he walks, roaring with fists waving in the air. He hates everything that spreads upward. He flattens seedlings and flowers with as much relish as he swats down insolent trees and stony crags. With bitter tears streaming down his face, he stamps down the mountains.

He has never allowed himself to cry in the name of his parents, but has cried helplessly as a child does, whimpering with no control or knowledge in the world; he feels that perverse release which is not a true release. It is a sadness which blackens the air and fills the eyes, nose, and mouth with soot. When he cries, he feels the thickness of his body and the dispassionate world around him begin a melding together. He lets himself blubber openly, believing or intuiting that, if he could only be consumed with sorrow — become a black hole of sadness — that the whole world would blend to a single coherent thing. Unity would have justice, would not allow the terror of life nor the murdering of parents. Unity would bring everything to equality.

This vision of justice and his severe drive for equality makes 2 Leg destroy. To others, he seems a mere monster bent on destruction, but truly he is full of a dream of fairness. It is a dream he can never understand well enough because of the death of his parents.

It is a dream he feels in his body as surely as one feels an idea. When he walks out to tear down the hills, the blackness slowly leaks throughout his limbs like the tensing and flexing of muscle. Sorrow entwines with that dream of justice to create a ring of weight in his chest. The center of this ring is a lacking, as if a giant thumb has pressed a bruise and suddenly released the pressure. This ring radiates a pulsing ache in the front of his shoulders and the tops of his knees. Throughout it all, there is a throbbing in the small of his back. But when he sees a mountain, hill, or tree, his heart beats faster. Then 2 Leg feels the pain in his back disappear. The ring expands outward to his wrists and ankles, and the very center is the turning of blood in his gut.

"Goddamn you!" he roars at whatever rises up. Language is dendrites and their systemic exchange of electrochemical impulses. Language is the discoloring of flesh, the blood-gorged limbic system, the crawling of skin at the back of the neck.

When he stamps his feet, the mountaintops crumble.

And often, as if to prove the unfairness of life and the torment of existence, birds fly up from the roiling dust. Instantly, the ring constricts, the vacancy aches in the center again, and the pain of his back spreads from his calves to the peak of his head.

Then he weeps.

Language is the word *love* buried behind too many neural exchanges, behind the self-deceit of his crying. It is a vast landscape with dust turning up in the wind, a vermilion sky. It is his father's face looking sideways while gently breathing. It is his mother's eyes, her smiling face against his father's neck. Language is all this and the air through his throat, the constriction of muscles, the shape of his body, and "O" bubbling forth amid tears.

For a long time, 2 Leg stays in the swamps, going out every day to equal out the pain and injustice that has spilled everywhere. Each day he goes further. The ring in his chest expands, then contracts, but never goes away. So he leaves.

He goes northward because he has shattered a mountain and a green cloud of birds scrambles that way. He screams at them, his arms flailing impotently, but they fly on.

Lumbering northward, he sees the earth turn colors beneath his feet. Above, the sky swirls vermilion, blue-black, suddenly turquoise. He walks.

Leagues out, 2 Leg surprises a covey of quail. The birds burst forth, skimming beside the weed entangled arms of 2 Leg, snipping the air with their small beaks, screaming at him in fear. He swats three down, but only manages to capture one of the small birds.

2 Leg holds the bird tightly in his hands, the tiny head rubbing from side to side over his fingers. Despite the roughness of his hands, 2 Leg can feel the nervous muscles twitch and the rapid beating of its heart. It is a rapid heartbeat which he understands. A short "tzip" comes irregularly from the bird's throat, and the eyes blink frantically.

2 Leg stamps down the shrub where the birds hid. He looks up at the sky,

but the other birds have long since flown away.

He feels the circle of emptiness disappear from his gut, and the muscles of his buttocks relax. The bird stops moving its head and only the eyes, muscles, and heart twitch; 2 Leg opens his hand so the bird's side is exposed between his fingers. He lifts the bird and strokes the feathers against his coarse cheeks. He holds the creature under his nose. He smells the sky tucked there among the wings and sees the slowly rolling clouds move across the bird's eyes.

"It isn't fair," he says.

The sorrow moves across his throat and belly like the flush of blood after breaking fast.

He closes his eyes and holds the bird's chest against his forehead. The heart beats fast as rain.

"We must all be alike," he says, holding the bird against his eyes.

He draws his finger across the animal's face, stroking backward from the beak. He rubs downward over the frail neck, the trembling wings. He pushes just slightly the rubbery belly, then guides his finger between the twig legs and down to the knotty knees. He tries to feel and know the minuscule nails of the toes.

"It isn't fair," 2 Leg whispers.

He pinches the head until the skull collapses. Fluids spill over the back of his hand. He pulls a wing from the body and rubs it over his chest as if it were a leaf. He pulls the other wing free and rubs it up and down his bare legs. He pinches off the pulpy head and lays it beside the wings, then he carefully snips down the torso with the tip of his teeth.

Opening the bird's breast, he captures the fluids along his forearms, then scoops the bird over his nose, eyes, and mouth. The fluids run down his forearms, and he rubs them over his own body. He closes his eyes as he breathes the inside of the bird. He licks the red cavity. He shudders. He licks against the wet and fleshy insides and shudders. He swallows the small organs that pull free under his probing tongue. He brings the flesh down to his neck and rubs the warm blood around his throat.

"Ungh," he says, and shudders.

He licks and bites the flesh within, then places the remains over the wings and head. 2 Leg rolls face down over the dissected bird, and he shudders.

When he stands erect, the muscles of his back feel rubbery, the inside of his eyes calm, and the quivering of his belly dream-like. In this trance, he walks northward, where the earth turns against the sky. When he sees the white earth licking upward like waves, he feels the tears swell in his eyes and a curious calm in his spine.

"Mother. Father," he says.

The words are like a child's new words. His speaking makes his skin crawl with pleasure. There is a hidden power in the words.

For a time, for a long time, the pain of unfairness leaves him. But, eventually, the calm of the bird leaves him too, and he walks with the vacancy of his belly accumulating anger.

There in the north, 2 Leg discovers how to capture birds. He fills bushes with salt, places lime on branches, and sets tar across feeders. Once captured, they fall to his cruel investigations. Boiling the live bodies, he discovers their methods of screaming. He sees how their bones move to carry their plump weight, how a finger has extended to give them flight, how hair coarsens into feathers, how the beak of a lizard hides inside each bird. He sees this and breaks his finger by trying to extend it. He coats his head with mud and allows the stinking entanglement of hair to harden. He eats the bird's raw bones. He eats their twitching wings. He pushes their mangled bodies into his mouth and jumps from trees to fly.

When all this causes not one bit of change, 2 Leg grabs the birds and fills their stomachs with stones. He pulls out their feathers and covers them with grass. He removes their legs and lets them roll in the wind like tumbleweeds.

Yet they multiply faster than he can kill them.

▼

"He is merely looking for nourishment," K'ux Kah says. "But to him black is everything."

The two sons understand this.

"It is already the end of him," they say to K'ux Kah.

So Jaguar Sun and Blowgunner strap on their pouches and fit blowguns neatly into cinches across their chests. They put bracelets around their ankles and wrists. They don headdresses. Each puts a jade pendant in his ear.

Following the roars and dust clouds, they track 2 Leg in the north. When 2 Leg sees the upright intruders, he bellows at them. He raises his arms, but the heroes merely pretend to be shooting birds.

"Who are you?" 2 Leg asks.

"Hunters of the plain," the two sons say.

"Leave me alone."

"We are passing while we kill birds," Jaguar Sun says. "We are only passing through."

"Kill them, and be gone."

"What are you doing?" Blowgunner asks.

"I am doing nothing. I am felling mountains from the path of light."

Blowgunner smiles at 2 Leg. "Yes," he says, "the birds we take increase the light."

2 Leg grunts, his tangled body like a bush in the wind. "Who are you?" he asks. "I don't know your faces. What are your names?"

"We have no names," Jaguar Sun says. "We are merely hunters of the plain. We hunt birds. We chase them through the mountains and bring them to the plains."

"There's a mountain rising further over there," Blowgunner says, pointing. "And there weren't any birds that we could catch up there."

"You couldn't have seen a mountain anywhere near here," 2 Leg says. "You're mistaken."

"No," Jaguar Sun says, "we have seen a mountain that is bigger than all other mountains. Perhaps it's grown since you last saw it. Perhaps you missed a little of the thing when you stamped by and it has since grown back."

"Impossible," 2 Leg says. "Where is this mountain?"

"At the sunrise."

2 Leg spits on the ground. "I shall end it."

The two sons are pleased.

"Take up the road with me," 2 Leg says to them.

"Only if you walk between us," they answer.

Jaguar Sun explains. "We shall practice our shooting."

Blowgunner shouts because he is happy for the chance to practice.

"Lead, then," 2 Leg says.

He is amazed that the two sons do not use pellets to kill the birds, but instead use their breath to bring the birds down. Well before reaching the mountain, the twins have enough birds for a feast. 2 Leg is sent to bring more firewood.

They build a fire to roast the birds and to raise a smoke up to the heavens. They cover the backs with the gypsum white earth of the mountainous north. "When the smell of the birds reaches him," they say, "then he will eat the birds cooked in earth, and he will die buried in earth."

2 Leg smells the flesh of the roasting birds. He smells the grease sizzling in the fire and sees the birds cooking to a golden brown. 2 Leg approaches the fire and lets the smoke rise up into his face.

"This is wonderful," he says. "How is it that you cook birds?"

"We cook them to eat them," the sons answer.

"It smells delicious."

He closes his eyes to enjoy the smell of roasting flesh even more. He opens his eyes to revel in the charred flesh spit over an orange-red fire.

"We cook all meat," Jaguar Sun says.

2 Leg shudders.

"This is fine," he says huskily. "Oh, this is very fine."

"Eat," Blowgunner says.

2 Leg takes one of the birds from the two sons. He holds the stick in both hands as if it is a lover's token: holding it close to his chest, his elbows pressing into his sides, his face mooning over the blackened birds.

The two sons stare at him, feeling a certain affection for 2 Leg's innocence.

"Eat," they say again.

2 Leg rubs the side of his face against the cooked bird. He lifts his hand to his cheek and slides his fingers on the grease. He rubs the bird over his brow and other cheek, enjoying the slipperiness of his face. His fingers glide effortlessly.

"Grease is white," he says excitedly.

The two sons stare.

"This is good. Very good."

"It is nourishing," Jaguar Sun says.

2 Leg's face brightens. "Yes."

He smiles at the sons, then puts the entire stick and bird into his mouth. He chews open-mouthed so the flavors permeate his throat, his nasal passages, and rise up to his eyes. Bits and pieces fall from his lips. Bits of the wood, pieces, stick to his teeth. He shudders and drools.

"Our Lord, K'ux Kah, just wants the remembrance of what he has created here on earth," Blowgunner says.

2 Leg stops chewing.

"It is just like your longing," Jaguar Sun adds.

2 Leg swallows what remains in his mouth and wipes an arm across his face. "You know nothing about me," he says.

"It matters what you love," they answer. "It matters what you praise."

2 Leg eyes them, recognizing slowly that they are his enemies, though he doesn't know why. He feels the familiar pain encircling his groin, tightening in his back, and the freshly eaten bird setting up a poisonous roar in his stomach.

"I am Destroyer of Mountains," he says, doubling over in pain.

The two sons of K'ux Kah look down at the dying 2 Leg.

"There was a mountain inside you," they say.